NOUMENA CONT!
# THE POPE'S LI
### by Friedrich Chr
**Translated by Robert A. Cantrick**

Rome, 2011. A German archaeologist and part-time tour guide accidentally stumbles upon the pope attending a Protestant church incognito and enters into a whirlwind of speculation: What does the pope's hand do when he's doing nothing? What might make his hand twitch? Is there such a thing as a papal slap, and if so to whom should it be administered? To the lecherous Italian Prime Minister? To a certain Libyan oil dictator as he curries favor with the Italian head of state with thirty Berber horses while at the same time attempting to convert all of Europe to Islam? And speaking of which, why did Saint Augustine have to bribe the Roman Emperor Honorius with eighty Numidian stallions to gain acceptance for the doctrine of original sin? Why do Germans long for Rome, even though—ever since the Teutonic invasions and the Nazi occupation—they have been considered the worst sort of barbarians there?

Meanwhile, the narrator's sister-in-law dreams of being pope, the pizza breath of noisy tourists wafts through the Sistine Chapel, and rats swarm about Via Veneto.

Looking past the idealized Rome of picture postcards, the tour guide mentally roams through the city's long history and extols the Italian art of saying yes and no at the same time.

At once a timeless tale of Rome and the birth of a modern legend: how the pope became a Lutheran.

### Praise for the German language edition

"A wonderful story . . . here a free spirit vents his feelings on the oppressive perfume of the Roman historical superpower."
*Süddeutsche Zeitung*

"A slender, intelligent book . . . satirical and written with literary finesse."

*Westdeutscher Rundfunk*

"Besides the *Baedeker*, this book belongs in the luggage of every visitor to Rome."

*Deutschlandfunk*

# THE POPE'S LEFT HAND
## by Friedrich Christian Delius

Translated from the German by Robert A. Cantrick

Noumena Press
Whately, Massachusetts
www.noumenapress.com

Noumena Contemporaries are published by Noumena Press
Manufactured in the United States of America by Sheridan
Set in Palatino Linotype
Printed on acid-free paper

Originally published under the title *Die linke Hand des Papstes*
Copyright © 2013 Rowohlt Berlin Verlag, Berlin

Version 1.0
ISBN-13: 9781733630108 (paperback)
Library of Congress Control Number: 2019934417

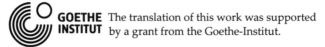 **GOETHE** The translation of this work was supported
**INSTITUT** by a grant from the Goethe-Institut.

Edited by R.J. Allinson
Cover design & interior layout by Rachel Thern
Cover art © 2019 Noumena Press

Frontispiece: altered detail of *La topografia di Roma* (1748)
by Giovanni Battista Nolli & Giambattista Piranesi

Also available as a PDF ebook
Visit www.noumenapress.com for details

## *Acknowledgments*

The translator wishes to thank his patient and generous friends, who, whether they volunteered to read drafts of the entire manuscript or offered advice on specific passages, gave unselfishly of their time and knowledge. Without the sharp eyes and literary acumen of Terese Bergfors, Robert Dees, Heidi Heigel, Joanne Pritchard, Rosalind Pritchard, Cheryl Pruitt, Mick Wadsley, Eva-Maria Wiesinger, Marklyn Wilson, and Sebastian Wohlfeil, this translation could never have attained its present quality.

I am particularly grateful to the anonymous denizens of the LEO online dictionary and forum, too numerous to credit individually, for their wise and perceptive insights into the intricacies of the German language.

The author himself was kind enough to read through the final draft of the translation and offer suggestions and corrections.

*For Vanda, Alberto, Peter*

As the truth about Rome is nowhere to be found, I dare to hope that the reader will forgive me for making a few brief observations. . . .

Stendhal, *Roman Walks*

The hand, I thought, on the first Sunday in March of 2011—what is it about the hand? Open, slightly curved, relaxed, hanging from the black sleeve, the fingers loosely beside each other, pale and effeminate, what does the pope's hand do when it's doing nothing? We spectators hear much about this man, whether we want to or not. His faces, his robes, the windows that serve as his stages are shown constantly, every Sunday you can hear him sing, speak, and bless, every day thousands want to be filmed or photographed with him, he is quoted everywhere, his violet smile is sold on postcards, his power implored, sought, doubted, his role loved, valued, or scorned—but his hands, we know nothing about his hands, what about the hands?

No, I was not surprised to see him so near, a few meters to my right, almost beside me, in the last row of the sanctuary, the elderly gentleman who by general agreement is called the pope. He was dressed unobtrusively, not in the regalia that proclaims his authority, no gold shone, no lilac, no crimson, his head, known the world over, was neither adorned with an imposing miter nor covered with a cap; he looked like a simple parson or bishop in plain clothes, with a black suit and starched white collar. To his right and left sat two priests, whom you might see near him on TV, in similarly neutral, plain attire. Gestures, looks, posture, everything was well rehearsed. The only disconcerting thing was that the three black-clad men were doing nothing and did not move forward, into the center, where they would have been more broadly visible.

Sitting in the same row with them, the aisle between us, my perspective was not the best. Since I did not want to make a spectacle of myself by gawking, I turned my head to the right as little as possible, peering over only discreetly, and I glimpsed the familiar face only fleetingly, in profile, between the faces of his escorts, six or seven meters away. That is why my eyes turned more toward the hands, toward the left one, mainly, the one closer to me, on his thigh, on his knee, on the backrest, or supporting his head. The right one was completely visible only when the elderly gentleman moved that arm and extended it forward a bit. The hands drew my gaze, and it was the presumed tiredness of old yet still-powerful hands that I began to contemplate. And the inactivity, to which they were perhaps not accustomed, for once not being used for one of the centuries-old rituals of his office and rank, not raised in greeting or to bless, not pressing other hands, inking signatures, turning pages, praying, holding wafers or liturgical vessels. Resting hands, pausing hands, the hands of a so-called infallible, unemployed for these few minutes, they invited me, they provoked me to reflect, they enticed me to discover the secret, if in fact there was a secret, that made them hang so noticeably soft and limp from a stiff body. They asked me riddles.

They seduced me into palm reading from a distance, you would be right to reproach me for that. But what else is a respectable heretic to do if he is afflicted with neither the blindness of the kneeling nor the arrogance of the church hater? What else is there for an archaeologist in premature retirement, who occasionally hires himself out as a tour guide, if, by whatever convoluted combination of coincidences, he has the opportunity

2

to observe a pope at close range, to savor the anecdotal moment quietly, not knowing whether the encounter will last half a minute, half an hour, or longer?

A study of the hands at a short remove, for me that was nothing more than an occupational habit, cleaning an object with brushes and, from the details, drawing conclusions about the object as a whole, then, with the whole object in view, checking every detail again and again. We're simply an odd mixture, we archaeologists, inquisitive potsherd cleaners, layer and fold interpreters, imaginative and meticulous, Latinists and utopians, as half-educated in history as we are in geology, homebodies, tent sleepers, dust eaters, detectives, and virtuosos of disappointment. We have only leads and details to go on, we have to bring loads of patience to a daily jigsaw puzzle with nothing but missing pieces, three-dimensional riddles that no one has yet solved. So, too, I scrutinized these hands dispassionately and professionally, trying to combine what I saw with what I knew and with what seemed likely in the great Roman mosaic, as some call it, or puzzle, as I call it, or, as one could also say, in the wonderfully disorderly pile of historical fragments, often described, always there to be rediscovered.

The hands aroused my curiosity but not the unusual location in which this encounter took place, which other observers might well have found strange or shocking. What business had the head of the Catholics in a Protestant church in the middle of Rome? I didn't ask myself that question, I could detect no sensation in it because this was not his first visit to this space. It was right here that I had seen him approximately one year earlier, but then it had been with full pontifical splendor, with closed-off streets, police lines, helicopters, ambulances, a limousine, guest lists, ID checks,

3

bag checks, metal detectors, jam-packed pews, excited whispering, a processional with retinue and thundering organ, crimson or green robes, I forget the color, his standardized and measured smile amid solemn Protestants, shaking hands with children, innumerable cameras, microphones, a gold-lacquered theater chair, pious hopes, a papal sermon from the Lutheran pulpit, and tact on all sides.

It was a diplomatic affair, a courtesy visit in remembrance of his Polish predecessor, who twenty-seven years earlier had been the first pope to set foot in a Protestant church, this very one, in Via Sicilia. My wife, Flavia, and I had sat approximately where I was sitting now. A lovely production it was, a gentle spectacle to mollify well-meaning Protestants dreaming of church unity or equality, whom he scorned, as we knew from other sources. He'll never forgive you for your five-hundred-year-old act of disobedience against the fraud of indulgences, Flavia said afterward, laughing, he needs you guys so that he can keep putting the blame on you for splitting the church. Why do these Protestants' eyes light up when they are allowed to shake hands with him—with *him*, of all people!

So it did not surprise me to encounter the prominent visitor here again. I might have asked myself why he turned up in this place for a second time after such a relatively short interval, but I gave the question no thought. The images of his official visit were still so fresh in my mind that I felt no excitement or awkwardness about this apparently unofficial visit, without papal armor, almost incognito. I thought only: Make good use of the unexpected audience, look at the hands, what is it about the hands?

The organ droned in the background. The man who had assumed the role of pontifex did not behave as though he were the center of attention. It seemed to me that I was the only one among the thirty or forty present giving him my undivided attention, unobtrusively, from the corner of my eye. He was sitting almost on the fringe, looking on and keeping silent. No cameras were pointed at him, neither the television recording machines carried on shoulders or mounted on tripods nor the heavy artillery of reporters, not even the handy camera phones you otherwise see held up on every street corner, in every church, every museum. Here no one was filming or taking pictures, and that alone lent the scene to which I became a witness on that Sunday before Rose Monday, Shrove Tuesday, and Ash Wednesday something agreeably old-fashion, even surreal.

There are sights more exciting than the pope in profile, and I felt little inclined to stare at one side of a milky, careworn face. I just peered over at the partially shaded hands, hanging, resting, supporting, on their fingers no sign of the ring that his subordinates and the devout are wont to kiss. Turn on your brain camera, I commanded, point the zoom at the hands. Think of painters, who make sketches before they stretch the canvas, mix the oils, and reach for a brush: sleeves, cuffs, each finger, every joint of a slightly curved hand, every nail bed, the creases, the veins. Think of the tensely curling fingers of Raphael's Julius, of Titian's hand of Paul III, of the letter in the left hand of Innocent by Velázquez. Note carefully what you see, I commanded myself, even without a pencil.

I had planned the afternoon of a tour guide quite differently. While Flavia, after a meeting at Lake Como, was taking the bus to Milan after about two p.m., then the express train to Rome, I had intended, before leading a group from Heilbronn, to take one more stroll through the city by myself, not having to play explainer and pseudo-all-knowing answer giver, without eager German listeners and their much-too-tight schedule, which they've recently started calling a window of time. I had intended just to follow my nose without the great Roman Jupiter Symphony in my ears, the allegro of motor noise, honking, car alarms, construction equipment, the rattle of motor scooters, dogs barking, the counterpoint of seagull calls and telephone calls, the crescendo of aggressive, stinking, or methane-tamed buses clattering over potholes, the andante of jostling on the black pavement along trampled tourist routes, the abrupt stops and ceaseless evasive maneuvering on zebra-striped crosswalks and photogenic stairways and in front of fountains, the slow tempos between souvenir shops, before columns, at tables of cheap goods, the dissonances of waiters in front of restaurants croaking in English to recruit customers and of black-skinned vendors shouting "*Capo!*" and selling white socks.

On Sundays, only the little symphony is on offer, andante cantabile, Sundays are more boring, but only on Sundays can I give my thoughts free rein in the city center, discover details and expand my knowledge, wander aimlessly through the realm of stone, which on the seventh day is not so bustling, clogged, noisy, and beset by traffic as it is on other days. Facades are not blocked by trucks, cars are not as slow and close, beggars restrict the range of their activity to church steps. Only on Sundays can one sit outside in front of the bars and not be immediately pestered by Africans selling Kleenex and fake handbags, Bengalis with fake watches and Chinese toys, Romanians with fake songs. On this Sunday I had only one objective, to get to the place where I was to meet the Heilbronners by five, at the

6

finger of doubting Thomas in Santa Croce, my favorite relic, as I say to amuse my more or less un-Christian friends and acquaintances.

A day for a Roman walk, another stroll from north to south through the whole Villa Borghese Park, delighting in the most beautiful women in the world without having to see them framed and banished to museographic order. I jilted them, left them in the Galleria Borghese, just retrieved a few paintings and sculptures from memory, the series of wonderful creatures, the Daphnes and Danaës, the Sibyls and the great Circe, the various deluxe editions of Venus, the ladies with unicorn and swan, Proserpina and Paolina, and then the dancing Satyr and the horny Apollo, Flavia's favorite god, placing his left hand so tenderly yet with such possessive determination on Daphne's hip and stomach, vainly trying to hold onto the beautiful girl as she flees the realm of the senses and turns into a laurel tree. I had walked past the bright facade of the museum, aware of the panorama of divine and earthly love and worldly pleasures behind it, commissioned by wise cardinals or popes, strolled under pines and dying palm trees, down pathways and over meadows and had created my own gallery of these magnificent women: Brescianino's Venus alongside Correggio's Danaë, Bernini's Daphne, Fontana's Minerva, and Titian's Sacred One, images that I could not forget, could not thrust from my mind, even now, when I found myself surrounded by conventional decor, beneath a golden Protestant mosaic heaven from the period of the First World War, in the unexpected and unaccustomed presence of a pope.

Not two hundred meters from Titian's *Amor Sacro e Amor Profano*, a woman of perhaps sixty, who must once have been very beautiful, repeatedly yelled "*Amore!*" at

7

her hysterically yapping dog, and only when I was past her did I see the comedy of it and in that moment began to wonder. Her face, it looked familiar, could that have been the Sandra or Alessandra or Alexia with whom, decades ago, during my first internship in Rome, I had sat on the steps of Sant'Agostino half the night talking about God-knows-what and whom I followed when the clock struck two? Definitely a mistake. In the exchange of glances between us, while the amore animal was barking at my legs, there would have been at least a tiny moment of embarrassment or awkwardness. Forget it, I now decided, no brooding about the past, please, no amore nostalgia, it was just an older woman who was once young, as I once was.

Woman with dog, an everyday and familiar scene, a talking symbol for the new dog cult. I could give whole lectures about it: Rome going to the Dogs and the Expulsion of Cats in the Transition from the Twentieth to the Twenty-First Century, The Tenfold Increase in Dogs in the Last Fifteen Years, The Dog Craze as Index of Italy's Decline. That's how far I could have taken this silliness if talk of decline were not already an Italian commonplace. Except that the wretched condition of the date palms had nothing to do with the decline of Italy; the insatiable red palm weevil immigrated from Spain. But what did I care about that beetle? I tried to force my thoughts back into the church where I was sitting and had set myself the modest task of concentrating on only one object: the left hand.

But the images of beautiful women that I had called up only moments before continued to run in the background, hard to control and not to be restrained, as though they wanted to defy the papal presence. And Lord Byron refused to be shoved aside either. I had just visited him at the southern end of Borghese Park on his pedestal with the verses, "Fair Italy, thou art the garden of the world. . . ." The poet, captivated by his own lines, gazes down Via Veneto, taking possession of the city with his enthusiasm, "Oh Rome! My country! City of the soul!" An ur-tourist, a tireless dreamer, who, from the filthy Rome of the early nineteenth century, from the dull dictatorship of priests, fabricated a Garden of Eden and paradise for souls. Byron's poetic pathos missed the mark back then and corresponds still less to today's realities. For that very reason I liked him, with his aloof, almost ridiculous pose, his narcissistic intoxication with Rome.

On this afternoon, too, reading those verses engraved in stone, I had envied them again, the Romantics and all who came after them, who were able to rewrite the world into a garden and idyll for themselves and cultivate the beautiful misconception that the foreign soil on which they stood was meant for their personal emotional satisfaction. Tourists, antitourists, and my enlightened tourists who travel for education, in every one of them there is a sight-seeing enthusiast, a history enthusiast, an arcadia seeker. On Via Veneto they want to think only of la dolce vita, breasts, champagne, and sports cars, of the formula or fiction of la dolce vita, which existed at best only for a few years or only in one movie. Every one a would-be Goethe, every one a dreamer, every one clings to his clichés and collects what fits them—I understand it well. Who, for example, wants to hear that this famous street was once the boulevard of the Nazi occupiers and today flourishes as artificially as it does thanks to the Casalesi and Russian Mafias, which doesn't keep the rats from paying their respects at the twilight hour. If I can bring myself to say: Look at that hotel over there, it was once the Hotel Flora, where SS murderers lived in luxury and the Roman resistance set off a bomb, though not as successfully as they did in Via Rasella, and so on, then the faces grimace. Nazi terror in the Eternal City? That kind of retrospection spoils the vacation mood. People prefer to read today's murder stories in crime novels or enjoy them on TV, see them set in Iceland, Sweden, or the Eifel rather than behind glorious facades and the inscrutable faces and gestures of waiters on Via Veneto.

People want to rhapsodize. Once hard-earned euros have been put down for flight and hotel, they want to bathe the soul in clear light, see it reflected in a cloudless blue sky, they want to experience the postcard views of ruins and sunsets behind umbrella pines on location, they want to taste the warm air and cooling pistachio ice cream and have the guide steer them to what is supposedly the best ice cream in Italy, they want the fairy tales. People want the palm trees, not the palm weevil. After all, you go to Rome to hear fairy tales, and on Via Veneto it can be only the fairy tale of la dolce vita—Swedish breasts, champagne, and Italian sports cars included. In the forum they need a kindly Caesar and antiquity as heroic epic, or, under St. Peter's Basilica, they want the ready-made legend of St. Peter's bones. Nowhere else have so many legends and myths been invented, and, because they've been repeated thousands of times, they miraculously become all but indistinguishable from the truth. Nowhere else, I say—though, I must admit, I know only Rome and Bremen—are people so eager to believe fabrications and so ready to let themselves be deceived as they are here.

Sometimes I envy them, the foreigners I guide, because they do not know and do not need to know what the police tell the press every now and again after someone is gunned down in the streets: which neighborhoods are controlled by the Calabrian Mafia and which by the Chinese, which by the Neapolitan, Casalesi, Romanian,

10

or Russian Mafia gangs. They even give the names of the families involved and their spheres of influence and put maps of the city in the newspaper with their names. Mafia-free zones seem no longer to exist in the "city of the soul," which obviously bothers no one in the land of a reigning friend of the Mafia. Sometimes a murder helps to achieve reallocation of turf and consolidation of supply routes; the garden of the world is staked out and divided up, "fair Italy" a battleground for business people—not exactly known for fairness—in the weapons, drugs, gambling, prostitution, human trafficking, extortion, and blackmail sectors. But here is my dilemma: visitors to Rome do not like to hear allusions of this kind; only when it's rumored that the Vatican is engaging in money laundering do people prick up their ears. The church and capital, that's always a big draw.

The most beautiful women, the handsome Byron, the amore woman, the elegant Veneto, the veiled Mafia, it surprised me how rapidly each new image faded in over the last, how rapidly my brain processed the simultaneous showing of these fresh impressions while I tried to get used to being in the presence of a pope. Clearly I did not want to be distracted, least of all leave the awkward, unpleasant field of Mafia associations, the minefield before which everyone immediately cries out: Careful! Cliché! Italy cliché! As enlightened, prejudice-free Europeans we are supposed to avoid that. Fighting preconceived notions has become the highest virtue, higher even than fighting the Mafia, which people like us can fight only by not remaining silent when everyone else is silent, by calling by their names whatever or whomever the police call by their names. The more these gangs spread out over all of Italy and half of Europe, the greater the Mafia's share in the proceeds of every tomato, every orange, the stronger this taboo becomes and the more strenuously everyone objects.

Please, don't demonize the Mafia, whisper the friends of the Mafia. Please, no pistols-and-pasta clichés, say the Italians. Please, enough of stale prejudices, cry the Germans, we're not sauerkraut-eating Huns, and they aren't spaghetti eaters, enough already!

Lately I've paid less attention to these taboos, sometimes at the risk of driving off what few clients I have. Tell your tourists this truth, too, Flavia advised me recently, the Mafia's heart beats not in Palermo, Naples, or Milan but in London. That's where it's easiest for our Italian clans and others to become fine business people with the dirty money they're allowed to bring in, unaudited and untaxed. For once you can praise our investigators, who run up against their limits with the good, financially compliant Britons. A wise piece of advice, that, London as paradise for European economic criminals. That really frightens my tourists, and I no longer have to spoil their Italian mood.

It was with digressions such as these about "fair Italy" that, after leaving Lord Byron, I had walked down Via Veneto, turned off, then, in Via Sicilia, saw the open doors of the Lutheran church, surprised that any doors at all were open at this time of the afternoon, let alone those of a church, when almost no one is out and about and families that gathered for lunch are just having their *caffè* or calling for the check in restaurants. I had entered, although there was nothing great, nothing particular to marvel at, no highlight, no must-see, no not-to-be-missed; at most, for Danes, there is the baptismal font by Thorvaldsen. I leave this church out of my tours, I had not been back here since that papal visit a year ago. Sit for a few minutes, that's all I wanted to do after being repelled by the pretentious coffee bars on Via Veneto and the looks of the uniformed waiters, reminding me of my worthlessness. The open doors and hard pews seemed just right for continuing to reflect upon how best to broach ugly truths with my clientele more gently, without being a spoilsport, a Rome spoiler.

After taking a seat close to the door and soon thereafter discovering the high visitor and his escorts, only gradually was I able to shake off the previously collected images and ideas and savor the minor sensation of sitting so unexpectedly close to the most famous man in the city, he on a splendid but no doubt unpleasantly cold marble pew, I on a wooden pew, likewise in the last row, only six or seven meters away. Who would ever expect a pope to forego the pompous entrance with entourage that is customary on such occasions and quietly take a seat in the background, humbly, without the consecration of flash units? The figure I had seen so often from a distance interested me little, a silent pope was another matter, and, finally, I was ready for the distraction. For a while I did not need to struggle with Mafia, Nazis, and the perils of rhapsodizing about Rome, and I remained sitting longer than I had intended.

It certainly would have been more exciting, our accidental encounter, if we want to call it an encounter, had it happened in a less unlikely place. If in a so-called house of God, then in a touristically and art-historically more exciting church, the Santa Maria della Vittoria, for example, not ten minutes from here, with Teresa in the throes of orgasm, or San Clemente—where I would have had much more to tell, could have indulged in vivid fantasies, incidentally doing some educating on hidden meanings and Roman stratification, from the Mithraic cult to the Totti cult—a church from the time of the invention of original sin. There I would have shone as tour guide, there I could have done some self-promotion on the sly as well, competition is stiff in our trade.

There are dozens, hundreds of places more attractive for meeting a pope, more attractive at least as a backdrop suitable for television images and vivid colors for shaky, blurry proof of authenticity on YouTube. There was still not a camera to be seen, no flashing pocket phone. I was not thinking of future proof, either, I was not thinking even of writing a first-hand account of this Sunday afternoon, of the necessity of writing one, because the unheard-of event of the day had not yet happened. If from the beginning I'd had any inkling of what I was about to experience, my observations, instead of being fixed only on the elderly gentleman's hands, certainly would have been somewhat more broadly conceived.

Even that might not forestall possible objections by future readers of these lines: If you're doing an exclusive on the pope incognito in words and words alone, some will think, then please, Saint Peter's or the Lateran or Santa Maria dei Miracoli as the backdrop, or revel in baroque! Can't you rewrite your report, delete winter, celebrate spring, have blue sky instead of a closed Protestant interior? And while you're at it, churches are a bit much anyway, couldn't you choose a photogenic corner of the Forum or the Baths of Caracalla for your meeting? Go to the popular Pincian Hill with its vista and evening sun, couldn't you meet the disguised pope on a park bench there?

If I want to stick to the truth, I have to forego such excursions, pretty postcards with rosy sunsets, pandering to expectations, offering art prints. I did not choose the setting. Can I help it if something drew the pope to this space for a second time? I can't just move him to Santa Maria della Vittoria. And I have to report as accurately as possible what I saw, heard, felt, and thought before I got to the climax of the day, the sensation of the year.

I would gladly have changed the venue, exchanged the Protestant interior for a Catholic one, but the elderly gentleman with the gentle, tired look remained seated, almost motionless, on the marble pew. If I want to stick to the truth, I can speak only of this comparatively homely church, about which there is little to tell, a product of the last years of Wilhelm II, with much marble and strained mosaic work, not ugly, but with little aura, scarcely any history, no scars.

So my eager eyes concentrated on the hands, as the archaeologist in me had learned to do. First, take in the overall picture, then carefully expose each layer one by one, in this case from the fingers to the hand, from the fingers to the cuff, to the sleeve, then position, coloration, wrinkles. Draw further conclusions about the find and its stratum, in this case without ruler, notebook, pencil, or brushes, with only imagination and estimation, step by step, beginning with the left hand on the left knee. An archaeologist does not excavate, that is a misconception, my professor taught us in the first semester, an archaeologist frees the eye.

Writing hands, I thought, of course, those are writing hands, the right one presumably the writing hand, the left one the assisting, paper-holding hand. Slender, powerful hands that, by what they sign or do not sign, can make many things happen with three or four loops of ink under letters, decrees, bulls, encyclicals, or whatever else there may be in the arsenal of papal power to command and his sole right to interpret. No small amount of power to strengthen one soul or another and mitigate suffering in front of one or another African or South American household shrine. But I didn't want to develop that line of thought, and before imagination tempted me with everything that a signature from this hand could change, I commanded myself: Don't start in

15

on the nonsense about what you would do if you were king, if you were chancellor, if you were pope! With difficulty I managed to fight off such childish omnipotence games, but, as I sat on that hard pew, the harder I tried to fight off the temptation to usurp the office of pope in my own mind, to encroach upon the Vatican's sovereignty, the more clearly the image of my Italian sister-in-law in Cologne intruded, who once said: If I were pope.

If I were pope, Monica said, I would advise the archbishop of Cologne and his canons to take heart or show some remorse and return the Shrine of the Three Kings to Milan. The archbishop wouldn't even really need to have a heart or feign remorse, she said, he could do it out of political, Euro-political, Catholic calculation, for marketing reasons, and return the Three Kings, stolen eight hundred years ago, to Milan—desecrated and plundered by Frederick Barbarossa—for, say, just the next eight hundred years. What a spectacle of reconciliation and unification it would be if the people of Cologne voluntarily offered to return the relics, Monica said, it would be not only in the spirit of all Italian and European patriots, it really would be a grand Catholic gesture, and in the process the Germans would gain respect, which could lead to a decisive improvement in strained German-Italian relations. That is what this stalwart Catholic said, this Italian woman from Cologne.

I tried to imagine the hands signing an instruction or proposal like that and at the same time thought of my sister-in-law's smiling face. If you were pope? I asked, What can I do to help you become pope? Ah, she said, a restitution like that is still too modest, not bold enough. Let us hope that in the twenty-first or twenty-second century people will be allowed to be a little more Christian, a little freer and not as fundamentalist as before, as today. If I were archbishop, I would say: We don't need the Three Kings any more, they aren't the Three Kings anyway. I would say to my colleague in Milan: We both know the facts, my dear colleague, in the Bible there's not a word about the Kings; only Matthew, nearly a hundred years later, gives us a nice story about the three magicians. Of course, we believe in these kings anyway, but we don't even know where they went, what became of them, in what corners of the Orient they died. All we know is that our diligent Helen, the eighty-year-old collector of thousands of relics, with her unfailing instinct, identified the magician's bones three hundred and fifty years later lying neatly side by side in the middle of Palestine, somewhere between Jerusalem and Bethlehem. Earlier, my colleague, I would say, we needed this humbug about those magicians and the myth of the holy deceiver Helen, who for good reason has a place in one of the four main piers of St. Peter's. We needed it earlier for our undisciplined, simple-minded faithful and as a city development program, both my predecessors in Cologne and yours in Milan. We in Cologne, at any rate, are now strong and devout enough that we no longer need such—just between you and me—such a fraud. Take this shrine, take it for the next eight hundred years, my dear fellow archbishop, do with it what you will. But at the hand over, let us have a great festival of Catholic charity and celebrate a break with fundamentalism.

And the gold in the coffered ceiling of Santa Maria Maggiore, I asked her, would you return that, too, to the descendants of the slaughtered Incas and Aztecs? No, she said, like every good pope, I would be a local patriot. That's how I recall the words of the Italian woman from Cologne, who since then has come no closer to her dream job, and again I sensed how much fun it could be to distort and mix up history with

17

what-would-have-happened-if fantasies and let my-self drift down the slope of figments like that. I pulled myself together and tried to put the brakes on my imagination and show the popesses and archbishopesses to the door of my brain's activity.

The organ fell silent, I had scarcely been listening, it had been playing only rather thin strains, nothing from the usual repertoire of Bach, Buxtehude, or Telemann. A man in dark attire, but not a cassock, stepped to the microphone and announced that today Shrove Sunday was being observed, *Esto Mihi*, which translated means "Be my rock and my fortress," the beginning of psalm number something or other, and he began to read it in a monotone. Be my rock and fortress, he intoned, and immediately his words mingled with the other pieces of the puzzle and the mosaic tiles, with the images of the afternoon flying through my head: the white hands of the elderly gentleman on the marble pew, the paintings of naked women and the rock metaphor of the psalmist, the marble hands of Byron and those of the dancing satyr and Apollo's hand on Daphne's stomach, the invisible Mafia on Via Veneto and the visible Sicilian, Calabrian, and Neapolitan ones in the two houses of parliament, and then the woman with the little dog in the Villa Borghese, the Holy Kings of Milan, the sounds of the organ that had just stopped, and the chirping of birds in the acacias outside. After my initial nervousness, brought on by the man with the face known the world over, I began to enjoy just being able to sit there, savoring the simultaneous show, letting all these colorful mosaic stones whirl through the nerve cells of my memory, mixing, turning, recombining.

The eyes of the people in the rows ahead of me were directed toward the front, where the psalm was being read, not toward the important gentleman in the last row. His face seemed shaded in the half-light at the back of the sanctuary, but only because it was not illuminated by the sun or floodlights, as it usually is. The pope did not want to be noticed. It was not clear to me whether or not the others had discovered that he was there, whether they were pretending to be more indifferent than I or were more absorbed in what the organ had offered them or in what they were now hearing. So far, no songs had been sung, no prayers spoken, no liturgical phrases murmured, but it seemed to bother no one that, on this Sunday, at an unusual, early-afternoon hour, the rituals were somehow different. The voice of the man reciting the psalm about rocks and fortresses and mightiness did nothing to make me want to listen more closely.

I stayed focused as an observer of the writing hands, which can move so many things in the world and now were not moving and, at the same time, in my mind's eye, I saw the left hand of Apollo, the seducer, the would-be rapist. That famous sculpture—chiseled, hewn, and polished during the Thirty Years' War, when Rome lent a powerful hand in the rape of Germany— is one of those odd simultaneities, one of those quiz questions with no answer: what do Apollo and Daphne have to do with the Thirty Years' War? The hands immediately provoked the next question: whether what I had noticed is true, that neither the writing hands of Innocent X, painted by Velázquez, nor those of his successors had signed and recognized the Peace of Westphalia of 1648 and consequently that the Roman church has been in a state of war with the Germans for more than three hundred fifty years.

Then it came to me, it burst into my mind, the memory I wanted—finally I knew why, from the very first second of our arm's-length encounter, I had thought: The hands, what is it about the hands? Now I realized why I was so fixated on them. I had already applied my imagination to them once before, exactly six months earlier, when, in front of the television, I had long pondered whether these hands, whether the right papal hand— I always assumed he was a right-hander—was still capable of delivering a slap in the face. Or was capable of a spasm that, if not checked, could become a slap or become at least a spontaneous, immediately restrained movement. Or whether the dignity of the office or the fatigue of age or a timidity spreading throughout the limbs not only prohibits any such reflex but deadens even the thought of one.

Half a year earlier, when the oil dictator from the other side of the sea had come to Rome for the fourth state visit within a year to celebrate unbreakable friendship with the friend of dictators who rules here and to conclude business deals, barely transparent government and private deals, when the oil dictator and Islamist lay preacher boorishly mocked Christianity and the church, which was going too far, even for a respectable heretic, I could not help thinking, as I sat in front of the television, of an impulsive movement of the papal hands: a slap, not for the guest, that would not be good form, but for the host, who showered his pal from the desert with compliments from morning till night in front of microphones and cameras.

How had the man sitting beside me on the marble bench taken the news six months ago, I now wondered again, that the reigning Libyan whoremonger, on the occasion of his state visit to the reigning Italian whoremonger—which you had to say if you wanted to avoid the language of self-censorship and diplomacy and allow yourself the luxury of coming close to the truth—had rented ten busloads of young women and

20

summoned them before his tent on the grounds of his embassy? Pretty and quiet is what they had to be, it was said, and content with eighty euros for being extras at a lesson on the Koran delivered by the dictator himself, inducing three of the young women, with or without financial aid, to convert to Islam.

Not just this mission and the conversion itself might have upset the pope and his advisors, I speculated, but the new form of religious prostitution, the fact that in the capital city of Christianity, at the drop of a hat, several hundred young women could be found who, for the price of a jar of face cream and a tube of lipstick, would stoop to serving as extras for the recruitment blathering of a preaching libertine. In the papal chambers, I imagined, age-old questions must have come up again: How holy is the holy city of Rome still? How sinful has the Babylon on the Tiber already become? How ominous the statistic that, in this city, only half of all children are still baptized and almost every second marriage takes place without the blessing of the church? How, from so lofty a vantage point, does one view the fact that today the dumbest geese willingly let their religion, if they have one, be mocked for a mess of pottage? And on top of that, a pope can still be so fortunate as to be insufficiently informed about the Roman Babylon, in which droves of thirteen-year-old girls are sent by their parents to plastic surgery clinics to have their faces tailored to market requirements and in which it not infrequently happens that mothers of employment-seeking young women offer themselves or force themselves or their daughters upon bosses or heads of personnel departments so as, by means of one or another sex act, whether with the younger one or the more mature one, to advance the prospects of employment contracts.

What might have been more upsetting to him than sadness at the mass venality of a once-Catholic people, I was sure of it, would have been a kind of anger at the fact that an Arab ruler and Koran preacher flies into the capital city of Christianity and, not far from the Vatican, has the temerity to declare Christendom insignificant and to call upon Europe to convert to Islam. And proclaims this message grinningly, urbi et orbi, before five hundred rented young women and voracious cameras and microphones. Some church representatives, few newspapers, criticized this insolence, but not the editors of the newspapers and TV channels of the ruling television mogul. His politicians, down to the minister of simplification, heard these words and, half-pained, half shrugging their shoulders, took them without objection so as not to put the oil dictator in a bad mood and endanger profits from highway construction, weapons sales, and the installation of digital networks in Libya. They dismissed the guest's religious zeal as folklore, while the government-compliant television networks and newspapers celebrated friendship and harmony between the dictator and the friend of dictators.

Back then, in August 2010, it occurred to me for the first time, and now I could reconsider it from a better vantage point: Doesn't the hand of a man like the pope sometimes twitch? Does he not feel an urge to defend himself and, if not to land a punch on the reigning hypocrite, the host of the uncritically celebrated oil salesman and Islamist lay preacher, then at least to deal or dictate a sort-of slap, or at least have his subordinates, the bishops or press secretaries, dictate one, a short, carefully worded and nuanced verbal slap and for once use those writing hands to defend himself against the crudest forms of insolence?

Is it possible, I now wondered again, that a venerable man, after such an exemplary rise to the highest rank he can attain, can still allow himself to be shaken by controlled anger and feel the natural reflex to clench his fist quietly, behind his back, or deliver a slap, at least in his thoughts? Does fear of the mortal sin of anger forbid even the twitching in his arm? Does fear of the sin of poor form stifle every impulse of this kind? Or must the indignation that I suspect, or an inkling of indignation, founder in the fluff of diplomacy, dissipate in back-room deals or the vague formulas of communiqués? How long must, how long can someone such as he turn the other cheek and keep quiet, despite the moratorium to which he himself gave his blessing? Despite the al-liance of his Italian bishops with the reigning harem keeper for the benefit and protection of both sides: the bishops won't get in his face about his criminal activ-ities and private pleasures; he saves the church taxes and gives it schools, teachers, and the laws it needs.

Yes, back then, in front of the TV, I had felt an odd sympathy, a brief, genuine compassion for the papal man: What does he do when his hand twitches? Are his hands tied? Or does he just feel they are tied? What means does he have at his disposal against a blas-phemer who is useful to the church yet thinks only of himself and celebrates himself, who at the founding of his Mafia-friendly party invoked the Holy Ghost, held himself up as the Jesus Christ of politics, and praised the dictator of Russia as a gift from God?

I didn't know then, I didn't know now, as I watched the elderly gentleman with the milky-violet face sitting modestly in the background, in genuine or well-feigned modesty and made only slightly more prominent by the marble pew. But I was certain that he and I, a never-retired cleric and an archaeologist who had retired early, despite a thousand differences and disagreements, back then in August, perhaps just that one time, had had the same thought: if a Christian head of state from a European country were to appear in Tripoli and distribute Bibles to five hundred young men or women and assert that Arabia and Africa must become Christian, or, if he were to put on a show like that in Mecca, because in this case Rome can be likened only to Mecca, and declare that Arabia ought, if you please, to convert to Catholicism, he would either be stoned or massacred by some other means or, at best, driven out with military consequences.

He, however, the proselytizing state guest, was pointedly praised by the foreign minister of his Italian friend and business partner. Such witty, folkloric comments about the Islamization of Europe should not be taken seriously. After all, the honorable dictator had praised Italy as the only European power to end colonialism. That's how the minister described it at the end of this memorable state visit, and the relaxed, peaceful hands, obviously little suited to slapping faces, reminded me of it.

Once I was into this train of thought, the images of the horses came back to me, thirty purebred Berber horses, which the dictator had flown over after himself, as you could read everywhere. Next to the horses stood the horse-faced foreign minister, one of the more intelligent of the television magnate's lackeys who, as justice minister, had gotten lawsuits off the magnate's back, as European Union commissioner had deflected criticism from Brussels, and who now was spreading his diplomatic mantle on behalf of oil and highway contracts, bank stocks, armaments, and shares in television networks and declaring into microphones: Folklore, like these magnificent Berber horses, it's all just folklore! And the reigning friend of the church repeated it, bragging about his good relations with the pope, as he always did whenever he was attacked by one or another newspaper or by democrats, as they did during this visit by the dictator with its equestrian and missionary highlights, which had put me in mind of long-suffering, patient, or twitching papal hands. And, for the first and only time, I felt a measure of pity for the old man, whose hands were tied by the very power they wielded.

The horses, purebred Berber horses, as they were always called, I liked the fact that they sprang in among my thought fragments at this particular moment as I sat on a hard church pew. They crowded out the beautiful women from the Gallery Borghese. The poet lord, the Mafia clans, the Roman dogs retreated. Now the horses dominated the scene, the flying, athletic parade horses that the Libyan dictator brought along on two airplanes so that before the state dinner, which, because of Ramadan, began only after sundown, they could put on the kind of show for the eight hundred guests and business cronies that one would expect from splendidly caparisoned show horses, trotting and cantering in smaller and larger, open and closed formations, in synchronized and sequential jumping, all of them feats by costumed riders on expertly trained horses such as one gets to see at equestrian festivals and the better horse auctions.

Thirty Arabian thoroughbreds and thirty aristocratically attired Bedouins are what the man who sneers at Christianity, democracy, and human rights mobilized so that he could bask in the applause of Italian politicians, entrepreneurs, and military chiefs at the Salvo D'Acquisto barracks. The government-subservient television network, which was also the

Vatican-subservient television network, presented—to me and perhaps even to the pope, who is known to be a news watcher—the two grinning robber captains in the most favorable light, in the center of the screen, flanked by delighted, applauding dignitaries, beneath the midnight Roman summer sky.

I recalled that, as I watched the broadcast, I found the episode with the Arabian thoroughbreds no less obscene than the missionary sloganeering, not because of its cost or the dictatorial whims, not because of the childish entertainment put on by the two ruling aficionados of horses' legs and girls' legs, but because of the horses themselves, transported from one continent to another as political advertising. They reminded me of something, these nags sent across the Mediterranean from North Africa, they gave me no peace, and at the time, August of 2010, it took a few minutes, maybe even half an hour, until the synapses of my brain pointed in the right direction: Augustine! Did he not gain acceptance in Rome for his theory of original sin with the aid of bribery? With a bribe of eighty Numidian studhorses, transported to Italy by boat?

In this report on my minutes with the pope on Shrove Sunday I do not want to pose as an expert on church history. I am an archaeologist and a one-quarter educated, half-illegally moonlighting tour guide, still awaiting the license promised me by the Comune di Roma. My meager knowledge is from "casual reading," as it is all-too-disparagingly called, picked up, gleaned, but read for all of that. Some of it I get from Flavia, the historian I married. All too seldom do I manage to retain certain details, such as this detail about the studhorses, discovered twenty years ago in a book on the theology of sin and original sin by a female theologian.

Horses, eighty Numidian studs, the price of the dogma of original sin! This is not the time or place to explore the childhood of the son of a Bremen government official, but one thing can be said in general: anyone who has been browbeaten for years by Christian hostility toward the body and the dictates of the Augustinian doctrine of sin can never forget it, this footnote to church history. I believe it was my sister-in-law Monica in Cologne who recommended that book. All the needless tormenting of Christian humanity for sexuality can be ascribed to the father of the church, Augustine of North Africa, the bishop of Hippo near Carthage, and one or two boatloads of horses. What an epiphany, what a stroke of providence, what a delightful insight!

After the oil dictator's horses pranced across the TV screen, I reached for that book about original sin and let it retell the story of Pelagius. Desiring a humanitarian Christianity, he made reference to the young Augustine, thereby incurring the wrath of the old one. Ladies and Gentlemen, I would say as a tour guide, to put it simply, instead of building the church on a foundation of poverty and ethics, in later years the saint wanted to build it on a foundation of wealth and power, including power over souls. His God wants submission, not that everyone should go to heaven, as the Bible says. Complex controversies, those, that the master of black-and-white thinking kicked off, the despiser of women, the demonizer of sexual activity, who at first had been an ardent lover and had his mistresses, then, as soon as he mended his ways and became bishop, declared women inferior and all humanity "masses of sin," with the argument that because every person is conceived in lust of the flesh, carnal desire is transmitted with the semen, and therefore all humanity is stained with sin in the womb, all sinned along with Adam.

Now I had an expert at my side, a little way off, on a marble bench, and I was itching to ask: Your great saint, driven by this logic, even slandered marriage and defended prostitution so that the power of passion would not ruin everything, do you recall that? Would it not have been impertinent to do so, I would have liked to ask that of this elderly gentleman, who was the ultimate authority on the subject and who had publicly chosen that saint as his role model. He was sitting within earshot of me; it was not clear whether he was listening to the psalm-reading about the rocks or meditating or dozing. It would have been a once-in-a-lifetime opportunity for a little debate.

But I didn't dare, I held back, I had just felt compassion for him because of the way he must have suffered from the shamelessness of the oil dictator and the chummy silence of the ruling gasbag, so I did not want to seem forward, though I certainly did not mean the question to be so. I was just curious about how much awareness and memory of historical detail there is in his circles. Above us loomed the muscular, mosaic figure of Jesus holding in his left hand the book of alpha and omega, the Bible, which, in the view of most theologians, except for an ambiguous half sentence by Paul, says nothing about the theory of original sin. I was feeling neither timid nor forward, I was not trying to prove or refute anything, I just could not switch off my curiosity, and I did not move, nothing but horses before my eyes, Berber horses and their predecessors, Numidian stallions, waiting to make their entrance.

Do you recall, I could have asked the highest cleric, or any other cleric, the arguments Pelagius used to call the concept of original sin into question? The argument with which Augustine, to put it simply, turned Christian doctrine up to that point upside down and elevated God to a sadist who had created nothing but sinners who, despite their baptisms and confessions, had to be punished? To condemn all of humanity because, according to the legend, the first two people violated a taboo, that theory does not accord well with the theory of God's righteousness, or what do you think? Complicated terrain, on which to this day theologians of all factions waffle and turn backflips. You're the expert, I could have said, don't you agree with the Bible that creation is good the way it is and that man was created in the image of God? That's exactly what Pelagius said, as did, apparently, the majority of thinking Christians back then. There were polemics, fights, even street fights in Rome over these questions.

Historical details flashed, sharp images, refreshed six months earlier. And I heard myself say, as though I, too, wanted to excel in the discipline of backflips: Augustine had his opponent, who wanted an ethical, humanistic Christendom, declared a heretic and excommunicated by the pope, do you remember? It was completely pointless that I, a ridiculous tour guide, began to defend the great Pelagius, but I did it anyway, because it bothered me that he was not heard back then and subsequently sent an apologia to the bishop of Rome, the pope. However, that pope died before it reached him, and his successor (I had to look that up as I was writing this report: Zosimus) studied the letter, absolved Pelagius, rehabilitated him on all counts, and warned Augustine and his North African faction to stop the sectarianism about original sin, to act with love, and not disturb the peace.

Pope Zosimus, I might have continued, tried to tame Augustine, remember? And what did Augustine do, he who had not yet been canonized? He flew into a rage and refused to heed the dictum that to this day is the foundation of papal power: Rome has spoken, debate is over, *Roma locuta, causa finita*. No, the dogma of *basta!*— which he himself invented and which soon afterward was shortened to those four words—he preached only when it suited him, after his act of bribery had succeeded.

Now the stallions got their grand entrance into world history. The cunning bishop did not submit to Rome, instead he turned to the emperor (I had to look that up, too: Honorius), who at that time was the true head of the church but who, in turn, was dependent upon his military commanders and much in awe of Augustine, who was a family friend. Military commanders, battle-scarred old warriors, cavalry officers, they love thoroughbreds, and a Numidian stud was the Ferrari of that time, what's more, a Ferrari that sired more Ferraris. So Augustine, it was 418, sent a trusted friend, Bishop Alypius, across the sea to Ravenna with eighty Numidian stallions. In what semester do young theologians learn about that? The emperor promptly issued an edict against Pelagius, banished him and his followers from Rome, and forced the bishop of Rome, the pope, who did not then possess the papal authority that later popes would have, to condemn the Pelagians. I'm summarizing, you know church history better than I do. A coup, all bishops had to agree to it, anyone who defended himself, such as Julian of Eclanum, was deposed, excommunicated as a heretic, banished, his writings burned, and original sin became law and was peddled as the doctrine of grace. Augustine did not even have to deny the stallion operation.

A key to the Occident: horses, the dark, curried beauty and rhythmic elegance of four times eighty cantering, jumping, trotting horses' legs. The most well-bred of nags, the price paid for the cruelty and arbitrariness of the doctrine of grace, as one could say to savor the joke deep laid in the matter. The glimpse into the abyss of the early fifth century had been worth it. I was surprised by the sinister portrayal of God and the deeply pessimistic view of mankind held by a father of the church, who declared that all other-thinking Christians and all more mildly disposed congregations were enemies and devils and had them kicked out of the church until there were almost no Christians at all left under his dominion.

Right after that state visit, when the oil dictator's Berber horses trotted and cantered across Italian TV screens, I had asked myself what I now asked again, after the pope's hands and slaps not delivered had revived the memory of the historic horses: In the history of the church, so rich in adventures, intrigues, and betrayals, has there ever been a coup greater than this one, with such consequences for every woman, every man in Christian countries? The noble saint and his theory of sin has probably meddled in the youth of everyone, here more, there less. In more than a millennium and a half, there has not been a life that he has not influenced or made more difficult, no matter how wise and profound he may have been in other respects. So many questions for experts, and now, quite unexpectedly, I was sitting beside one, who by his silence encouraged me to let each question sprout new sheaves of questions.

But it was a one-sided conversation, a monologue, that I was having under the mosaic ceiling, and I thought it might be fairer not to subject the elderly gentleman to such a dispute, especially on one of his rare outside appearances, and under a Protestant roof at that. My imagination was instantly willing to compromise. I pictured myself sitting with the pope, his escorts, and the studhorses at another location, on the top step in front of Sant'Agostino in Campo Marzio, in front of his saint's temple, in the springtime sun. My imagination went straight to the place where, decades ago, I had spent half a night talking with Sandra or Alessandra who, I was now certain, bore absolutely no resemblance to the woman with the hysterical little amore dog in the Villa Borghese. That aging beauty probably came to mind only because she provoked the question: how might the dogma of original sin have affected a woman like her and so deformed her life that she scolded her yapper dog with the highest, the boldest, the most joyful name two people can call each other—Amore!

Love of dogs, original sin, divine love, I tried to stay serious and heard myself saying to the black-clad men: Don't look so sad, it's really not your fault that your predecessor, Zosimus, had his arm twisted by a bribed emperor. Who is going to wax moralistic over such ancient history? All that interests me, I would have said, had I said anything, is whether you knew about this and whether—in case you noticed this detail as you were reading Augustine or someone pointed it out to you—you think the lesser sin, committed to establish the great one, original sin, is venial. And whether you keep a saying handy for such occasions, such as: the kingdom of God is within stallions, too. Even I thought of a saying like that a few weeks ago as I was traveling through the Umbrian countryside by train and was amused by the sight of horses on a paddock grazing and jumping obstacles on a small equestrian course and, typical archaeologist that I am, wondered by how many generations they were removed from the African stallions of 418.

The horses trotted more slowly down my associative pathways, and now I saw the hands with somewhat different eyes. They may have their power to point the way, their power to bless, but they did not have the power to erase this footnote, this thriller, from church history and no power to delete the history film that the oil dictator's jades had set in motion in my head and rewound to the fifth century. The hands, they could condemn books, they could dismiss historians, mandate or forbid certain research, influence opinions, and try to control thought, but they could not prevent my turning the stallions into a splendid key for deciphering the city of Rome. They could not keep me from letting my stream of thoughts flow nor from probing the ground beneath the finds, beneath the thirty and the eighty thoroughbred horses—stratigraphically, as we archaeologists say, layer by layer, beneath each surface discovering, unearthing, and recording more strata. The spade is wiser than the archaeologist, another saying from my first semester.

These hands could not keep me from continuing to think and dig according to whim and power of imagination and appreciating, image by image, scene by scene, what I, trained mole, tile counter, potsherd brusher, saw in my field research: eighty groomed, curried, trained Arabian quadrupeds with eighty mighty penises are responsible for the fact that for a millennium and a half Christian humanity has not been permitted to use its sex organs with the same easygoing lust, responsibility, and love as, say, Buddhist, Islamic, Jewish, or Hindu humanity. They, too, have their problems, but from us one wants to take away the central driving force, the beautiful driving force Eros, the ever-renewable energy Eros, the highest stage of civilized humanity, sold in Ravenna for a few purebred hacks, given to a few military leaders, one thousand six hundred years ago. Eighty magnificent studhorses, and we are guilt-laden masses of sin for all eternity. If that is not grounds for divine laughter: for us, lust and pleasure are supposed to be sins and the use of certain organs permitted only for feelingless breeding of sin-laden offspring, while eighty African studhorses sired more studhorses and purebred mares with Italic-Gothic mares, and Bishop Alypius, who brought the animals to the imperial court, enjoyed the benefit of beatification. And the pleasure of celebrating his feast day on the Assumption of Mary.

I was beginning to enjoy trying to figure out how as a tour guide one might recount tales from these strange events of long ago without giving lectures. How do you report events that are ancient yet have effects right down to the twenty-first century—today they're called scandals—without wagging the index finger of we who were born later at the iron fists and cruder methods of earlier rulers? How, while your listeners admire the blue sky overhead, do you bring up a forgotten Pelagius or Julian without getting lost in the insane fifth century? How, in an informal talk, do you cope with the difference in elevation between lofty saint and wily con artist? Or make the leap in the opposite direction?

Although I hardly needed it for my tours, I resolved to read up on why, in the times of upheaval around 400, the previously persecuted Christians became persecutors, the religion of the poor became the religion of the rich and powerful, and why Augustine's concept of sin suited the church and state so well and whether he could have rammed it through without the gift of horses. I knew a thing or two about the Vandals and Emperor Constantine, but now my archaeologist's curiosity was aiming far beyond its sphere of expertise. I knew too little, but then, even a tour guide doesn't have to know everything.

Soul management as core business, that was the next oscillation of my brain waves. Sant'Agostino in Campo

Marzio could become the pilgrimage church for psychologists and therapists, for the worldwide guild of more- and less-successful headshrinkers. All of them, of whatever school or tendency, owe it to the concept of original sin and to Christian people who have been degraded to masses of sin that they have infinite amounts of work, prestige, and income. It has enormous tourist potential and is completely untapped because Romans do not know the turning points in church history. Masses of educated people could be lured to the city and shown the sites where the tradition of intimidation, sexual oppression, and enslavement of the soul got its start—as a voluble tour guide might summarize it.

The more extreme and totalitarian dogmas like original sin are, Flavia said when I came across this wonderful subject after the oil dictator's visit, the easier it is to ignore them. As I sat in the pew thinking of her and wishing she were here to witness this unheard-of encounter, she must have been on the bus to Milan. Life, as she says every so often to encourage her German companion, the Bremen tax official's son, consists precisely of undermining dogmas, poking fun at ideologies, contradicting preconceived notions. We have the most experience with that, as you know, at least a millennium and a half of Catholic rulers. That really drills it into you. But, as always, we overdo it, we keep overdoing it without limit until we wind up with the opposite. Just look at our top mass of sin, why, he's even abolishing sin, he's freeing himself from all rules against sin and all ten commandments. He's sinned mightily against every commandment, against only one has he not, let's be fair, at least he honors mother and father. But there are few laws he hasn't violated.

That omnipresent individual—whom we too often do a favor by making him the subject of our gossip—now intruded even more impudently into my monologues, which had been about papal hands and slaps not delivered. But now, for the first time, a connection had been established. The reigning master of corruption, I thought, could also invoke Augustine's stallions, saying: Augustine used bribery to load those packets of sin onto you, I now set you free from all sin. I am Saint Anti-Augustine, I say unto you: There are no more sins! There are no more punishments! There are no more referees and no judges! I absolve you of all sin, even without confession! I'm buying you, so save yourselves! The more you think only of your own advantage, my people, the freer you will be!

On tours of the city, at some point, a few offhand remarks under the heading of corruption are always required. I usually take care of them at the palace of the ruling billionaire. Admittedly, the classic ones: Italy and crooked deals. You may yawn, Ladies and Gentlemen, nepotism, favoritism, clientelism have existed since the ancient Romans and popes, in every century. Cicero preaches vainly against corruption, Dante sticks rows of venal popes—who think too much of power and money—head first into hell and criticizes Constantine for his donation because, he says, it made the church wealthy and corrupt, and anyway the donation was a lie told by a covetous priesthood. Today the papers are full of scandals and revelations, but nothing ever changes, every outrage blows over in two days. The culture of venality is everywhere, of course, but not everywhere is it as highly developed, refined, and widespread as it is here.

At this point, nice German tourists like to exclaim: Stereotype! Prejudice! Old hat! Then it helps to point to the statistic that Italy is currently seventy-second on the corruption index, below Rwanda and Ghana, one place ahead of Georgia. And then it helps to refer to the sitting bribery artist, who is presiding over a continuing drop on the list. Italy has fallen to third-from-last place in Europe, just ahead of Bulgaria and Romania. It is a consolation to some if I add that Germany is slipping downward, too, not upward.

It's always a delicate point, but my principle is that I never say anything worse about Italy than do my Italian friends or my Italian wife, who goes so far as to call her country a rogue state, even on Sundays in the shade in front of a trattoria in the Sabine Hills over a plate of *bucatini all'amatriciana*. There are scoundrels everywhere, she adds, when we have guests from Germany, but I don't mean the little people, who can't afford strict legality. To be not corrupt presupposes a certain level of luxury. I'm talking about the well-off scoundrels, they're everywhere, but here, the ones that get caught are never punished, almost never. On the other hand, the minority, the halfway decent and cor-rect people, and there are more such nonscoundrels and antiscoundrels than you might think, are denounced by the big scoundrels as Taliban, Communists, criminals, or enemies of Italy, and that's what's different, at least from the democratic countries. And what's worse, this minority has lost all hope of ever becoming a majority.

Flavia, whom I pictured sitting on the bus to Milan, be-gins her lectures and seminars on Italian history for first-semester students by saying: Those of you whose parents pay no taxes or too little taxes, in other words, who contribute nothing for streets, schools, for heat in this lecture hall, for flushing your feces, and for my salary, please leave the room. I'll wait for two minutes. There is always a third of the young people who get nervous or turn red in the face and bravely remain seated. There's nothing more I can do, I can't collect the hundred thirty or hundred seventy billion per year in unpaid taxes, but they will remember that sentence forever. That's what Flavia says, the laughing citizen.

The watched, interrogated, and by now partially explored hands did not keep the reigning scoundrel from usurping ever more space on the stage in my head and refusing to be shooed away, the man we wouldn't have to talk about if he were where he belongs, where he would be if he were in any other country in Europe, in prison. He isn't the root of all evil, Flavia will have said once again to foreign visitors at dinner or during breaks at Lake Como, but he's the catalyst of all evil: fraud, balance-sheet falsification, lies, extreme egoism, privatization of policy, and abolition of the separation of powers. And he buys anything and anyone who is for sale, it's that simple. As long as he has the Mafias on his side, he'll be with us, and he has mastered the diabolical trick, against which even exorcists are powerless, of presenting himself as a loyal son of the church: "We never act against the Vatican."

He and Italy have an agreement, says my friend Antonio. They love each other. He has a philosophy of life shared by the people who elect him: What is life? Do well for yourself, think of yourself as much as possible and not of others, do nothing for society, for the state, just satisfy your own needs, says he. The spirit of modern times, of capitalism without limits, is this: promise to make people rich, and the Mafia take the hindmost. Those who oppose him have a hard time of it, one lie after another, dozens every day and everywhere, says Giuseppe, it's a deluge, you drown, and if you try to refute one and manage to get back onto solid ground, you get ten more lies the next minute, you can't keep up, you become resigned. Anyone who doesn't give up, like some journalists who write about organized crime, has to live under police protection. It's an inexhaustible subject, it just tires everyone out, *tutti siamo stanchi*, as Alberto says, because no one can get upset three times a day, least of all at the television set.

I, too, had long since become as apathetic as my friends and as fatalistic as a true Roman, and I might well have stayed that way on this afternoon had the hands of the elderly gentleman not reawakened my recollection of those slaps to the face never dealt and the little-known studhorses and Augustine's stratagem, had I not established the connection between original sin and the sins of the reigning master of ceremonies—via a route more labyrinthine than logical, I must admit. It's precisely when you ponder the ancient and modern variants of the art of bribery that you have to marvel at what a coup original sin was, an achievement of genius, as ingenious as Odysseus's Trojan horse. Everyone knows what happened to Troy, but no one wants to know what happened with the Numidian stallions, because it is as embarrassing as it is comical: a religion that condemns the great majority of its followers to hell.

With such divagations flashing through my mind I remained calm, even upbeat. I did not at all expect to see the hands of history turned back like those of a clock. What was done in the name of the church or of some emperor many hundreds of years or more than a thousand years ago by fraudulent means—which is what one would have to say by today's legal standards—whether for the lowest or loftiest of material reasons, are, as we all know, the salt of history, they are the foundations of power. A respectable tour guide would have little to talk about in the Eternal City, not as many facades and works of art, not as much carnage and beauty to show off without the many blessings of eternal corruption. "O Rome! Homeland of all vice," as

Alfieri wrote—a useful working hypothesis. And anyone who, with wrinkled nose and superior tut-tut, calls
that Rome bashing doesn't know Roman Rome bashing.

More entangling, I said silently to my silent conversation partner, are rather the ceremonial excuses that
your side makes: We admit that we have erred, we, too,
were and are fallible, many things were imposed that
by today's standards could be called illegal, but those,
we beg you to consider, were other times and had
other rules. What good are such confessions, softened
by the exhortation not to be bound by earthly truths
when there is the higher truth, the holy tradition, the
tacit agreements. Anyway, the superior attitude of
nonbelievers doesn't help anything, God moves in
mysterious ways, and to fulfill his great plans he uses
human weakness and passions, even if it is the passion of a few warriors for Numidian studhorses. On the
other hand, morality brewed according to Protestant
purity laws would be just as foolish as these lame,
soothing formulas, proclaimed only in emergencies,
with a weak smile, when facts can no longer be denied
and lies burst at the seams.

Whether it's studhorses or the Pantheon deal by the
unknown emperor Phocas or Mussolini's box of cash
in gratitude for papal acknowledgement that he was an
honorable statesman, no one today ought to fear free
inquiry into hidden histories. I could have called that
over to the three men in black in the next pew or on the
steps of Agostino. Even someone occasionally smitten
with the urge to ask questions and the stratigraphic
curiosity of an archaeologist wanting to educate and
entertain his clientele with a few anecdotes from by-
gone centuries must at some point stop the questioning
and scratching at legends. Even I can't say where the
questioning should end, but it has to end sometime,

when the answers become more and more alike. Ever since the serial killer Constantine placed himself at the head of the empire and Christianity, it's always been about—pardon the platitude, but in Rome two hundred years ago you would have been strung up or locked away for such platitudes—it's always been first and foremost about power and subjugation and only secondarily about faith and fear of God. If, with today's superior knowledge and legal puritanism, petty and fussy about your reputation, vindictive and historically blind, you were to ask about everything in the last two thousand years that does not merit the seal of approval by our constitution and Civil Code, everything that by today's penal code should have been punished, then, from what little I know, not much would remain of the three churches, Catholic, Lutheran, and Orthodox. We'd be more Lutheran than Luther, more Pelagian than Pelagius, more Franciscan than Francis, more Husian than Hus, more Brunian than Bruno, more Küngian than Küng. And people like Flavia and me would not be able to have fun with Numidian stallions and faked Donations of Constantine and could not enjoy the lecture by our friend Peter on the complete fabrication of the life of Francis of Assisi and the compulsions of a painter like Giotto to represent him as compatible with Rome.

My interlocutor on the right remained silent and flexed the fingers of his left hand. If you revive offenses for which the statutes of limitations have run out, whether you do it out of dismay, shame, or for tactical reasons— thus did my thoughts continue to weave the strands— then everything can get still more embarrassing. This pope's predecessor, for example, once tried issuing a loud, blanket apology, in the Holy Year 2000, for the persecution and torture of Jews and so-called heretics, witches, and gypsies by men and women of the church. After absolving his forebears of guilt, almost all of whom believed in witches, heretics, and Jesus killers and never felt the slightest guilt about it, he solemnly declared that the church, despite its hatred and policies, despite the persecutions and murders, the wars and burnings at the stake, extortion, raids, falsifications, bribery, and crimes it had instigated had for almost two thousand years, remained "immaculate."

Hundreds of thousands or millions of people killed in the name of the cross, driven out, tortured, and those who ordered this terror are immaculate. That, Flavia said at the time, you may call a miracle, a new Roman miracle. And a tour guide, who takes German tourists through the former ghetto, cannot help noticing that the beloved pope uttered not a word about the immaculate saint from Hippo who, despite his philosophical and theological greatness, turned the phrase "love thine enemies" on its head like no one before or since and saw nothing but enemies and opponents everywhere, preached hatred of Jews and heretics, despised women, forbade thinking, and campaigned for torture and holy wars. Remedial education on this is left up to people like us.

They led me far afield, these studhorses, took my associations on a wild ride to places where I did not want to go, where I did not know my way, they ranged over uncertain terrain. I should not have fixed all my sensibilities on the hands and the flashes of insight they triggered, I should have got up and left long ago. But I felt as though something were holding me in the sanctuary of this church, though it had not been my destination. I had intended to continue, I had been on my way on this Sunday, with a whole procession of images in my cranium, the beauty queens from the Galleria Borghese, the woman with her amore yapper, the pathos-Byron, Via Veneto with Nazis, Fellini, Mafiosi, and rats on the sidewalk, the oil dictator and his nags—who for the previous several days had been fighting the population of his country with heavy weapons and bombers. It was as though I were watching the synapses of my brain at work as they connected one thing to another, the yapper with the organ, the reigning goat in "the garden of the world" with the Westphalian warrior Innocence and the bombing preacher of Libya; Bernini with Ravenna, the steps of Sant'Agostino with therapists, and, in the middle of it all, time and again, the old hands, mysteriously connected to Rome's dark recesses, the dust of history, and to the innocence of this incomprehensible word immaculate.

Immaculate. You could get that idea only in a capital city of megalomania. Rome, I like to say, has lived from exaggeration and delusions of grandeur since April twenty-first, sevenfivethree. Romulus was convinced that the gods had ordained his few huts the *caput mundi*, or at least Livy succeeded in ascribing that belief to him. As an alternative, the navel of the world is on offer in the Forum. Even the phrase *Roma aeterna* is purely literary. Virgil has Jupiter prophesy eternal life for the city, and we parrot that to this day. The delusions of grandeur continued with the popes, who would be vicars of Christ on earth and as infallible as He himself, with the northern Italians, who moved in and made themselves at home with the Palace of Justice and the Unity Monument, those mountains of travertine and marble, with Mussolini, who staged his march into Rome on the date in October when Constantine won his victory at Ponte Milvio and then proceeded to wipe out half the old city. All the conquering boneheads, down to the Nazis, who thought they could rule the Romans with occupation and terror, all became megalomanic in this city. And today there is the harmless delusion of grandeur of the experts on Rome, ten thousand educated Germans alone, running around here believing they are connoisseurs, and I'm just one of them. That's why no one should be surprised that whenever anyone so much as hints at megalomania, Romans recoil and always first exclaim, "No!" then wait and do nothing and hope for a miracle. But you can't get by without megalomania here. You have to be strong and act important, modesty won't so much as get you over a crosswalk.

Here, disagreement reigns supreme, I say, when I have to play the expert, yes, Rome is the capital city of strife, everyone fights with everyone. There is strife between clerics and laicists, strife among clerics and between their orders, strife among laicists and between their parties, and the people who quarrel most bitterly of all are those who are ninety-eight percent in agreement. Strife between center and periphery, Fascists and Communists, the pious and heretics, Lazio soccer and Roma soccer, Raphael and Michelangelo, Bernini and Borromini, rogues and victims, those who look on and those who look away, the submissive and egomaniacs, Romulus and Remus. Everyone fights with everyone, there cannot be a conversation about an eaves trough without lawyers. Rome consists of the craziest mix of feuding couples, estranged brothers, the sharpest contradictions. A hundred invisible walls, a thousand invisible rules and pitfalls run through the city.

And the punch line, which hardly anyone knows about, probably not even the man whose immaculate hands I was watching, the most beautiful contradiction of all, is to be found where the popes are elected: in the Sistine Chapel. I have to confess, I have not set foot in the Vatican museums or that chapel in three years. Ten thoroughbreds could not drag me there, not even clients' tips. In double time through the galleries and rooms, here a glance at Laocoön, at the Raphael rooms, there at Apollo, here three, there four sentences of explanation next to seven other groups in five different languages, and, as everywhere else, there is more photography than looking, so who needs a tour guide? But the Sistine Chapel, where everyone wants to go, where supposedly all visitors to Rome must be able to say they've been, toward which everyone races, for me, it's the Sistine Hell. Tour groups jammed together side by side, in sandals in summer and reeking of sweat and perfume, in winter in heavy jackets, wet raincoats, and running shoes, under the Last Judgment. Twenty thousand people a day turn their faces upward, pumping the stifling, almost windowless, hard-to-ventilate chapel full of their vapors, of which their breath is the best part. You think you smell the mass pizza breath and see it seeping like mold into the frescoes below the creation of Adam. Then they take pictures, though it's not allowed, the attendants bellow, then they chatter and explain and interpret what they see or don't see. The loud murmuring is interrupted every three minutes by a guard shouting, "*Silenzio!*" Then it subsides and thirty seconds later swells again. Lately, loudspeakers demand silence nonstop in five languages.

It hurts me, conservative as I am, when violence is done to art simply because the church needs money and five million visitors per year. In the crowding, the stale air, and the drone of voices, no contemplation is possible, not even absorbing the most basic details. The great contradiction, which is left out of the guidebooks, would have to be explained in peace and quiet: here Michelangelo gives expression to his critical attitude toward the church. Instead of nice apostles with halos, as was expected of him, he painted prophets and mythical figures. Look at Maria, I would have to

45

whisper or shout, she turns away from the beseeching people and refers them to Christ, almost fearfully. And Peter is offering him the keys, the Vicar is no longer needed, at least not on Judgment Day. Please, Ladies and Gentlemen, I would have to shout, look at Hell, this Hell does not serve the usual fear propaganda. First, it is relatively small, second, many of the candidates for Hell are still permitted to struggle and hope for salvation, nothing there about Augustinian damnation for original sin, nothing there about a future in Hell for those who do not obey the popes. That's how a high-ranking Catholic once explained it to me. Michelangelo, as an adherent of early reformationist ideas, paints his critique of the church on the famous altar wall: the end of the papacy, of the cult of Maria, and of the menace of sin. The artist, Ladies and Gentlemen, never got over the fact that his closest female friend, the countess and poet Vittoria Colonna, was banished from Rome and branded a heretic for—to put it simply—reformationist, proto-Protestant views, both punishments inspired by writings that were subsequently deemed heretical and banned. Michelangelo they could not banish. Take a good look at the Moses statue in San Pietro in Vincoli, how defiantly he turns his head away from the superstition of Peter's chains. That's how art triumphs over dogma, that is the glad tidings, Ladies and Gentlemen. The irony of the Last Judgment, of the greatest and most beautiful of Roman contradictions is this: a near-heretic gives the papacy a gold mine that has worked for five hundred years! And, as a bonus, the perfect logo: the dome of St. Peter's Basilica.

It is in contrasts such as these, I reveal to the advanced ones, that you will find it, the Roman rhythm, the real beat of yes and no. Or in the crowding and hesitating in heavy traffic, in the simultaneous accelerating and braking in the tumult and jostling of battered cars. In the brisk whirr of Motorinis, the casual and vicious jousting among rolling knights for centimeters on black basalt, all against all and then back in flowing formation like the murmuration of starlings in the evening sky. When the density of beggars increases, when the buses don't come, the Metro, the trains, I, too, curse and rejoice in the faltering rhythm of the city, the conflict, the scolding, the tempers, the laughing, the sighing. Is it worthwhile getting upset at the sight of the mayor being congratulated with the Roman salute? At the sight of open trunks of police cars parked in front of the better stores miraculously filling with goods as if by themselves? At the ego games played out in fights over double and triple parking? Is the miraculous proliferation of official cars more important than getting a casual compliment in a bar? Is an amendment to an amendment of an amendment of a city ordinance worse than the fine Sahara dust on cars? No, it makes no sense to bang your head on these Roman rocks. Whoever understands that and finds the rhythm of these contradictions may one day attain the highest level of Roman wisdom: saying yes and no at the same time.

Sitting quietly on the wooden pew, I enjoyed these imaginary walks and leaps around the city, the wanderlust in my hippocampus, the restlessness of my brain cells. Never idle, they whirled through the archive in my head in microseconds, through the collections of images, sensory impressions, words, complete sentences, through the full yet ever-expanding arsenal of a tour guide and archaeologist who begins with hands and horses and ends up with Michelangelo, Motorinis, and Fellini.

The more quietly I sat, the more rapidly snatches from films of the fifties and sixties shot past me, images that had become ingrained, which is what made it so difficult to leap over fifty years and comprehend the harshness, gutting, and kitschification of the city today. At the same time, images of today surged toward me, and with closed, satiated eyes I saw rip-off artists dressed as legionnaires in the glare of floodlights, summertime discotheques in the Villa Borghese, multimedia shows of Roman emperors, brand new compact cars on display in the Ara Pacis of Augustus, one bar after another renovated in the metallic Milanese style. I saw Rome-born vandals, who previously had only smeared fascist slogans on facades, destroying the stone heads of famous Italians on the Pincio and knocking off the noses of Mazzini, Foscolo, and Dante, saw a happy-hour sign in front of every pizza parlor, saw the she-wolf on right-wing posters, baring her fangs, the Roman salute declared preservation of a tradition, and the fashion among the youth, aimed at their parents' taboos, of getting drunk in large groups or standing around, high on drugs, beside Giordano Bruno. I thought I could see it, the Rome of yore, the old Roman conviviality, the once-so-famous lightness, the easy sentimentality, the rough-hewn cordiality, the rustic humor, and the civic pride, disappearing into the noise, the filth, the snotty aggression, and sullen expressions. No ethics, says Flavia, no aesthetics, no culture, no money, everyone gets in everyone's way, Rome is not for sensitive souls. It's true that the Roman woman and the Roman man are generous, she says, but impudent, morose, lethargic, fatalistic. Dante sent apathetic souls to limbo, she says, because they failed to make use of their intellect and will, but Romans are indifferent to Dante as well, and anyway they feel like they're already in limbo.

Whoever who wants it, the feel-good Rome, should have it, Trevi and urbi et orbi and spaghetti on a side street in Trastevere included. As far as I'm concerned

"The Eternal City in Six Hours," too, better yet with the app, "Rome in Three Minutes." Head straight to the well-known, the overrun, the most-photographed places, to the Fellini photos and the postcards with the dome of St. Peter's in seductive evening light—away with the incomprehensible, the unknown, the invisible, ignore the residents of the suburbs, the beggars, the hovels, the crumbling stones of the fountains and the Colosseum, the stench of urine on the Spanish steps. All in Rome that's getting uglier, please take it with a sense of humor, like former mayor Argan: Rome is eternal because its decline never ends. And no one, I say, is obliged to be interested in the present. But please, do keep an eye on the future, on our Roman Chinese. For twenty years they have supplied the souvenirs of Rome, for ten they've worked in the souvenir shops, in the last five they've taken over whole tourist streets. You can already go see it: the dawn of the Chinese era in Prato, Naples, and on our highest hill, the Esquiline.

Educate the eye, wrote Stendhal, my role model as a tour guide. Anyone who has not educated his eye or does not want to will get no enjoyment from this city. A pedagogue I am not, but I try to direct the eye to things that are hard to digest and to conjure the ghosts that are still present everywhere, such as the ghosts of Constantine, Phocas, Pope Boniface—who did get slapped in the face—the anti-Catholic Michelangelo, the invisible Kappler, and the reigning Pinocchio. Or, at the Colosseum, I try to talk about the temple in Jerusalem that the Romans destroyed (my Flavians, says Flavia), after which they forced Jewish slaves to build this temple for gladiators, which today is the exclusive advertising temple of a shoe dealer because the semi-fascists in the city administration would rather line their own pockets than preserve tradition, homeland, and patrimony.

Educate the eye, even at the universally beloved Bernini elephant with the obelisk on its back. Some tour guides—I spent a whole day watching colleagues who speak languages I understand—still point out the inscription, "Let every beholder reflect on this lesson: it takes a strong mind to sustain solid wisdom, *solidam sapientiam sustinere*." But I know of only one colleague who challenges her customers with the solid wisdom that only after his triumphal return from Paris could Bernini get away with turning the elephant's behind toward the Inquisition building, where Giordano Bruno and Galileo and hundreds of other strong minds were tortured.

That brought me back to the three men of the church in my row of pews. I would have liked to ask them whether they could sustain small truths like that and whether they even knew the name Phocas, which none of my audiences ever has. Phocas, I say, with the intention of conveying ancient news to my customers with reckless brevity while making it as nuanced as possible, was the most murderous emperor in a line of late-Roman rulers that was not short on murderers, a captain who putsched his way to the top in Byzantium and exterminated the family of his predecessor along with hundreds of their closest friends. So nothing to get excited about, but among all the murdering Christian emperors, he is considered the most brutal tyrant, his epoch the bloodiest, his eight-year reign one of the most catastrophic in the history of the empire, and all of these harsh judgments, Ladies and Gentlemen, come not from me but from historians, even from Ploetz, who is reserved about moral questions. This universally hated tyrant had only one friend and admirer in the empire, Pope Gregory, the famous Gregory the Great, a competent manager, who looked after the Roman people and who also invented the legend of Benedict and the rumor of purgatory. So Gregory celebrates the murdering emperor as a messenger of God and a man of the Holy Spirit. The latter, flattered, though he is an Eastern Roman, acknowledges the leading role of the Roman Catholic church, calling it the head of all churches. Shortly after Gregory's death, Phocas comes to Rome, 608, in case you're interested. The new pope has a gilded column erected in Phocas's honor in the Forum Romanum, the last one to be built for a ruler, the tallest in the entire forum, over there, in the middle, unfortunately without the gold, now. Phocas is so touched that he gives the pope the Pantheon and sets his seal of approval on the Catholic Church as the head of all churches, a claim that it makes to this day.

That's approximately how it trips from my tongue on relaxed days. Audiences on tours for the advanced enjoy being regaled with tales of greater and lesser skullduggery from the past, they call it learning from history, and it makes them happy. The temple, I continue, gets rededicated as a Christian church, so the Pantheon was preserved, we owe that to the scoundrel Phocas. The wise pope seizes the heathen priests' idea of honoring all the gods in one place, has the martyrs worshipped here, and invents the Feast of All Saints. Everything is connected to everything, says Dante, so there certainly is a deeper meaning, Ladies and Gentlemen, in the fact that of all the columns, the Phocas column is not only the most recent and the tallest in the Forum, it is also the only one that has remained standing; all the others that you see here were rebuilt later. So much for the scoundrel's column, I say to conclude my four minutes of adult continuing education, and for the Pantheon as a gift of bribery. And that is why, to this day, some can enjoy the magnificent structure and others the church's exclusive right of representation, *caput omnium ecclesiarum* for the Mesdames Messieurs Latinists among you.

I glanced over furtively at my silent conversation partners, waiting, giving them time to object, but they seemed more silent than ever and remained motionless. The flashes of insight and mental images had flown by much too rapidly, even I could barely keep up with them, and only now, writing them down afterward, do I get them in order, into the drawn-out sequence of letters, lines, and pages. I remained thus seated, as though the galloping thoughts that the Libyan and Numidian horses had started required an antipode, outward inactivity. Flavia was in swaying motion on a bus, somewhere north of Milan, or already on the train, but I stayed where I was, shifting only my sitting position. Perhaps I felt no need for motion because I did not know or did not want to know whether I had been sitting on that wooden bench for one minute or twenty. I was only vaguely aware of what was going on around me, I was following the leaps and switching in my brain cells, paying attention neither to noises in the background nor to other people in my line of sight, glancing discreetly to my right every now and again, only the sound of the organ and the reading of that one psalm in my ears.

Only afterward can I say that I did not notice the passage of time, I did not look at my watch. At no point had I any sensation that minutes were passing nor that hours, minutes, seconds, tenths of seconds even existed. It was a quiet immersion in timelessness, in a stratum of time neither measured nor perceived as fleeting. It all seemed to me like a single moment, a moment that stood still, it was as though my first glance at the hand or the tenth, as though the dictator's horses and those of Augustine had drawn me into a sustained daydream from which I did not want to be aroused and which I did not want to interrupt by abrupt movement, by suddenly getting up and leaving.

And yet I was wide awake and knew, despite my look back at battles fought long ago, that in these months, the man whose hands I was observing had worries on his mind quite other than the education of pilgrims to Rome, other than the central sin and the horses from North Africa that go with it. He literally had his hands full with priests who could not control their sex drives, priests whose careers needed to be advanced, priests whose careers needed to be braked, priests trying to be more pious and devout than the Vatican, priests who objected to too much obedience, priests who falsified balance sheets, betrayed the church and made deals with crooks, priests who exposed them and got punitive transfers for it, priests who no longer wanted to be priests—a thousand pressing problems, questions, and decisions.

A madhouse. Now I remembered the word I had heard soon after that state visit with the thoroughbred horses in the summer of 2010. It was no church hater or disillusioned priest who said that about the Vatican but a high-ranking Dutch diplomat who had once studied archaeology with me and therefore allowed himself some candor, an authority sympathetic toward the most powerful small state in the world. A madhouse, he said, because the Infallible One is a weak leader, his secretary of state, too. Sometimes they work against each other, rarely with each other, faction fights rage, and in the middle of it all is the strongest and most intrigue-prone grouping, which presumes to be doing the "Work of God" and occupies more and more key posts. As an outsider, it is hard to tell at any given moment which of the lines and beliefs among the debating parties has the upper hand, what smoke bombs are being tossed behind which doors, what maneuvers, what muddy formulations are currently in vogue. The greatest fear is that some of this thrusting and parrying will get out.

Fighting, cover-ups, and kicking go on under the Holy See as always, but more ferociously now than in decades or centuries. More the diplomat would not say.

Maybe that authority was wrong, experts make mistakes all the time, and, I reminded myself, my perception could be wrong, too, yet the madhouse metaphor fit in with the fears I had come across so often among clerics in my twenty-seven years in Rome, above all the fear of not conforming to standards in a labyrinth of norms, dogmas, and legends, the fear of doing something wrong, of venturing one syllable, one gesture more than is allowed. Perhaps such fears flourished particularly well in a larger concentration of men under a mating ban, in a climate of caution, deference, and forbearance, where bodies in the service of a higher power are as though idled and are only for the display of imposing clerical garb, and hands are not permitted to pursue the truths of human warmth. Intense fear of the language of the body, repressed fear of happiness hormones, all kinds of explosive material. Such an aggregation of grown men, who stalk each other because at any moment there can be someone who suspects that a colleague is not as true to the commandments and as firm in belief, not as disciplined as oneself and therefore seems as damnable as enviable, that must lead to constant frictions and rivalries, more explosive perhaps than a classroom of pubescent boys. So I found the diplomat's concept, madhouse, quite fitting, even moderate, in view of the conflicting anxieties that must surround the elderly gentleman and in view of the air of sadness that I thought I saw in him.

But the madhouse didn't interest me. Intrigues among Catholic priests did not have to concern me, that was cheap fodder for journalists. Even if I were given permission to ask the pope just one question, I thought, not here on the pews of the church but at an official press conference with questions submitted in advance in writing, I would not be intent upon an answer to his problems with pious pedophiles or anti-Semites; enough words have been written about that. If I were allowed one question, I thought, I would not get into the madhouse of the present but the comedies of history. Then it would be appropriate to dig up age-old questions that always get shoved aside, such as the one on the mind of Monica, my Italian sister-in-law in Cologne, about Helen's talent for finding relics. Or I would want to know whether and when and in how many hundred years the Holy See might be prepared to admit that the famous Saint Benedict is nothing more or less than a literary figure, an invention by Saint Gregory or his disciple. I would also be interested in how many in the Vatican are aware that the cult of Mary became possible only because of two translation errors. Or, in the twenty-first century, for what ulterior reason state visitors, before an audience, are still made to walk through the Sala Regia, where murals celebrate the assassination of Coligny and the murder of the Huguenots ordered by the Holy See.

All these questions for the most authoritative and powerful of theologians might well have led to fascinating, perhaps bizarre answers, to masterfully evasive maneuvers, shrewd counterquestions, or whatever, but they would also have had something typically Protestant, self-righteous, or gloating, and I didn't want that, I didn't need it. Once the oil dictator had lured me onto the scent, the multifaceted image of horses in Augustine's game of intrigue had elbowed its way ahead of all others, the role of the horses in the calendar of saints. That is why I would have confined myself to asking whether, in light of this detail, in moments of meditation upon sin, original sin, and infallibility, those horses trot or gallop through the mind of the head of the church. More than that I would not want to know.

Of course I did not ask, neither aloud nor in a note passed to the right, I just watched my imagination at work as it piled question upon question, and, despite other flashes of insight, concentrated on just the one, on the ocean voyage with the distant, now dreamily blurred, now sharply outlined horses, on the wild ride through the forest of history with stallions. Of course I could expect no answer, the unassuming man sitting six or seven meters away remained unapproachable and, for me, inaccessible, and that was as it should be. My questions, I must confess, were more important to me than possible answers, I did not need to have answers. Rather, I was driven by an interest in finding out what exercises there are for forgetting, looking away, evading uncomfortable truths, what techniques one learns to dispute facts, to deem them unimportant, to keep quiet about them, to repress or hide them—an ability in church people, politicians, and other powerful people that I envy anew every day.

There was something I did not yet understand: why the talkative Italian people can also keep so perfectly silent, not only when the Mafias threaten or help, the famous Neapolitan silence, the Sicilian, the Calabrese, the Sardinian, the fascist silence. And above it all, the Vatican silence: the eloquent church, a master at keeping its mouth shut, of hiding, concealing, covering up, of amnesia and narcosis when facts threaten to become painful. As though they were trying to confirm what brain researchers have discovered, that inquiring thought inhibits faith and that religious people are less critical and less able to deal with uncertainty and conflict than people of lesser religious conviction.

The Catholic silence, an infinite subject, too large for a retired potsherd duster and puzzle lover, who also remained silent and, instead of getting up and addressing his silent conversation partner, stuck to his resolve to discover the secret of two hands.

If the hands are not capable of slapping, not allowed to be, what is the handshake like? I asked next, and visualized the visitor, now so quiet, as he had appeared in this place a year earlier when he appeared in full pontifical and pressed so many hands. I had wondered whether it was firm or limp, that handshake, brusque, tepid, or fishy, rather more caressing or intended to maintain distance with practiced, deceptive force. Semifirm and short, I did not think the hands hanging from the black sleeves capable of a grip like that. I supposed instead the lukewarm and fishy variant that I had noticed so often with clergy. That could be explained by the chastity or lack of experience of these hands, which as a rule have never been permitted to develop sensitivity for touching. Hands that have never stroked another person's skin with the tenderest yet most deliberate of movements, hands that have never cradled a neck, buttocks, or breasts, index fingers that have never ventured even as far as the foregarden of the feminine Eden, heels of hands that have never been bitten, fingers that have never been caressed by a woman's tongue, how capable could they be? It was hard to imagine the power to strengthen souls in hands that have never explored another body or have touched one only with a trembling fear of being caught in such sin and stopped short of the loveliest ecstasy. For these hands, for these men, separated from their bodies, one would have to feel compassion had they not of their own free wills abandoned the wisdom of the Greeks and Romans: that Amor and Psyche, physical love and emotional warmth, cannot be separated. Apollo's hand

57

on Daphne's hip and stomach, I thought, and hands bred to be chaste, that therefore suffer poor circulation, that renounce the fireworks of endorphins, what a contrast! Praise be to Cardinal Borghese for having had the wisdom to commission Bernini to transmute that contradiction into gracefulness.

How are hands like that supposed to find the right pressure and the proper grip in the cruder outside world, I sometimes thought when a weak handshake made me shudder or when I thought I saw others giving one, as I did a year ago, when the man now staying in the background extended his hand to the Lutheran minister and the parish councils, perhaps giving them a small surge of pontifical pride that they can brag about to the ends of their lives in a more or less pleased tone of voice: I once shook hands with the pope!

I once shook hands with the pope, my uncle Helmut said, who, as a soldier, not yet twenty, in the middle of the war, happened into Pius XII. He wanted to become a doctor, did so later. In 1942, medical NCO in the air force in Como, in charge of caring for wounded soldiers, he had to travel to Rome on official business. Before his appointment at headquarters, he's walking around the center of town, in uniform of course, and goes into Vatican City, St. Peter's Square, a foreign country, off limits for soldiers, and he doesn't know it, but there are no barriers. He gets into a conversation with a German chaplain, who asks if he'd like to be in an audience with the pope. They go into an office, the chaplain gets him a document for admission that says—though he's only an NCO—*Ufficiale*.

Which is why they put him in the front row. About thirty people are present, they all fall to their knees before the pope, kiss the ring, he, as a Protestant, gets up, clicks his heels, and salutes. Pius asks him his name, rank, where he's from, he knows the area in the north of Hesse, where Helmut is from, talks about a hospital in Kassel that he visited often as nuncio. Then the great pope says to the little NCO, "You're fortunate to have such a leader," shakes his hand, and asks if he'd like to have a gift. So he gets flustered, the young man does. What is he, a Protestant, a German, a soldier, supposed to want from the pope personally? "A picture, maybe?" he asks. "Yes, a picture of you would be really nice," says Helmut (of course, he didn't really mean it, he admitted when he told me about it), and at the end of the audience he is handed a postcard with a photo of Pius XII.

What brings the supreme leader of a church, in front of a nineteen-year-old German NCO who just happens by, to laud the biggest criminal of the twentieth century, a man regarded by the whole world in 1942, except in the German Reich, as a dictator, anti-Semite, warmonger, and murderer, saying he's a "fortunate" thing? I've often asked myself that, and my uncle, who said that even back then he avoided the Nazis as much as possible, asked it many times as well. Because it looked as though the so-called führer was putting an end to Bolshevism? But to extol him voluntarily, unequivocally, and half publicly, that was going quite far. It vexed my uncle, and it has vexed me ever since I saw that photo and heard the story, which, however, as I learned from Flavia, complements well what historians independent of the Vatican have discovered about the forties. Sometimes I think perhaps that's the reason I was drawn to Italy and to my profession, perhaps that's the reason I became a history sleuth, a surface scratcher, a potsherd prospector, because so important a pope spoke this sentence to my favorite uncle, the good-natured doctor, because I wanted to find out how something like that was possible beneath the innocent blue sky of Rome (but those are personal speculations and out of place in this report).

To get back to facts: now, on the church pew, I did not want to think yet again about that dreadful statement about the führer but about the handshake. What might the handshake of Pius have been like? I didn't ask my uncle, and now it was too late, now I could only guess. The Pius handshake, I speculated, might well have been firmer than that of his successor sitting here. Guesses, conjectures, preconceived ideas, I know, but they kept flying through my head, faster than shooting stars, no sooner thought than gone, as I listened to the voice of the psalm reader, unable to summon any interest in the individual words and sentences. For the left papal hand made an unmistakable movement for the first time. The fingers stretched then curled into a fist several times in succession and finally relaxed, as though the emphatic movement had alleviated a cramp or relieved an unpleasant twinge in the joints, some minor discomfort.

Peering to my right, well into the driving beat of my brain cells alternating between my uncle's hand and the hand of Pius, I sensed that I had less control than ever over the blizzard of thoughts, that they were drifting away, into the darker side of history. I tried to slow them down, but in fractions of a second they veered toward war, occupation, Wehrmacht, SS, raids, the deportation of Roman Jews, swept past the murder of hostages and the well-known and less well-known crimes, made straight for reports of terror and gruesome images, images both photographic and vividly described, that, once in your eyes, are not quickly driven out.

In the next-to-last moment, too late, that is, I tried to focus on the psalm reader's voice, but from his words, "Pull me out of the net that they have laid privily for me," I could not quickly form an image powerful enough against the trucks bearing down on me. At the very last moment, too late, I tried to mobilize the women, to summon the beautiful women from the Galleria Borghese to block out the Nazi filth, the German terror buried deep in the rubble of Roman memory, as if Apollo's hand restraining the fleeing Daphne, an alluringly lascivious Danaë, or any one of the Venuses could drive from my mind the awful images of the men in their trucks standing before the Vatican.

Yes, when is a person master of his racing thoughts? I was not, in these tenths of a second, and neither the psalms nor the women had the power to stop the men storming into my mind as I watched from the safe distance of a daydream. At the edge of St. Peter's Square, where the broad oval of its columns opens onto the junction with the Avenue of Conciliation, of reconciliation, of the Lateran Accords, there they stand on a rainy October day, 1943, four or five trucks with grey-green or black tarpaulins over their backs, in front of a low iron fence marking the city limit. They stand with hoods and front wheels toward church and dome, exhausts to the Tiber, toward the Mausoleum of Hadrian, not drawn up in military formation at regulation intervals and right angles but irregularly. At the steering wheels, in the front seats, young men in SS uniforms, youths playing the tough guy, boneheads permitted to play at being the elite, well-educated accessories to terror and accomplices in murder. There they sit, behind the windshields, and look at the fountain with the obelisk, at the facade, at the world-famous dome, the colonnades, they let the motors idle, a one-cigarette break, they marvel, they stare, they smoke.

That's how eyewitnesses reported it, eyewitnesses who knew what freight was behind these young men in the cargo beds of their trucks: people, packed together, wedged in standing, ordered from their beds, their homes by shouting, armed Germans, fifteen minutes' time, throw a few articles of clothing into a suitcase, something to eat, onto the cargo bed in pouring rain, one after another, ever more tightly crammed, women, men, infants, children, old people, many in nightgowns, a coat thrown over, shivering, dumb with fear, screaming in fear, sobbing, moaning, shut up in darkness under the heavy black canvas. That is how they were driven through the city, standing, swaying, crisscrossing, with no apparent destination, into the unknown, and finally, a stop.

A stop, we gather from reports and documents, because the young men in black uniforms wanted to relax for a moment after carrying out the first part of their orders: comb through houses, drive out occupants, load onto trucks, let none escape. That's called a raid, they rehearsed it, they executed it as directed, no incidents to report. All they have left to do is deliver their freight to a barracks up the Tiber a piece, but that part of the orders can wait. You don't know your way around Rome, so you make detours, and you can say you got lost because there are so many bends in the Tiber, because of the narrow streets. Driving is fun when you're lord of the land and have carried out your mission, the hardest part of the mission, and can allow yourself a few detours, a little tour of the city, past the gigantic, imposing, white marble monument. On Via dei Fori Imperiali, as the victorious commander, you wave at the Forum, at Caesar Augustus, at the triumphal arches. You gotta say you drove around the Colosseum and saw the Mausoleum of Hadrian and St. Peter's up close.

The men behind the windshields are stationed north of here and arrived only yesterday for this mission, they have never been to the city that people call eternal and may never return. For six weeks the Wehrmacht has occupied Rome, the Greater German Reich has been waging war on the Italians, whom they regarded as traitors because they are not as stupidly obedient as the Germans. No one knows how it will end, the Americans are already in Naples, so you have to make good use of every minute in *bella Italia*, in eternal Rome. They're on duty but also want to be tourists, at least for five minutes or three, for one cigarette, in front of the greatest church in the world and the most beautiful dome in the world, a symbol, the center, a landmark, even for SS men passing through. They don't have cameras with them, or maybe they do, they store the sight in their memories so that at home they have something to tell their brides, their mothers, their buddies, and maybe even the priest, something real heroes can brag about: I saw St. Peter's dome, and I almost saw the pope, too.

On the hard church bench, in a completely different epoch, I realized again that I could not simply block out this scene, which takes many thousands of times longer to describe, feeling my way, than it took to glide across the nerve tissue of my harried brain. A secret that I dragged around with me. A piece of the puzzle from the great puzzle of Rome that I do not want to force upon the foreigners I guide. A tour guide with a dark vision will lose first his customers then any prospect of getting the permit from the *Comune di Roma*, promised a year ago, still not issued.

I had to accept the fact that I could not get the snapshot on the fringe of St. Peter's Square out of my head, even when masses of tourists and pilgrims were milling about there, and not just because of the young men but because of their prisoners. On that October morning they quickly saw where they were, there would have been rips or small holes in the canvas, a tiny opening is enough, a Roman doesn't need a dome to know where he is: St. Peter's Square. That's a hope, almost a rescue, and so the tightly wedged people call out for the pope, they cry for help, summon the strength of their combined voices. At least one of the priests who usually walks by here, busy church people in small groups, by ones and twos, someone will alert the pope, they hope.

Penned up and persecuted by Christians for centuries, that doesn't matter now, now only he can become their savior, their neighbor, their shield, as they have believed ever since Mussolini, since Hitler. They are among the oldest Romans, their ancestors settled here, right on the Tiber, before the first Christians. They cry for help, they have been betrayed, three weeks ago they were required to pool all their gold, fifty kilograms, to be safe from deportation, that's what the Germans, Kappler, the top SS man, promised. They scream, but their cries can barely be heard above the idling engines, they do not make it even to the middle of the square, let alone up to the pope's study, not even if the window is open. Even if by chance he were standing right there, at best he would see the trucks so close to his border, not an unusual sight in occupied Rome, might shake his head at the disrespectful Germans, and turn back to his work.

Here the apparition broke off, the short St. Peter's Square sequence that has haunted me so often, among other things because of the dull cynicism or naïveté of the young accessories to murder. (Maybe, I think as I write this report, I can't rid myself of these young men because I see them as unusually perverse tourists, warriors as ur-tourists.) Granted, I did not like the fact that the point on the square, approximately where the trucks must have stood, at the junction with the Avenue of Conciliation, has since been renamed Pius XII. Nevertheless, I tried to persuade myself, these images, stronger than my power to switch them off, had nothing to do with the man on the marble bench, but that was not true. Maybe my defenses were so weak precisely on his account, because the hands whose pressure I was contemplating at that moment were on the verge of rewarding that predecessor—the one who referred to Hitler as "a fortunate thing"—with beatification. These German hands, no less, were trying to offset that pope's undisputed aid to victims of Nazi persecution against the disputed story of his so-called silence and his indisputable assistance to Nazi criminals. The impending elevation to sainthood bothered me for the additional reason that the television networks and the television despot, in preparation for this sacred act, had already made the life of Pius into a kitschy drama at the expense of the murdered Jews. And because, once again, only the Jewish community protested, again to St. Peter's Square, again completely alone, and again unheard.

The question was already lurking: why has the insane idea of Augustine, a father of the church, that all Jews are responsible forever for the death of Jesus, continued to have an influence through the centuries, establishing for them a kind of original sin with the punishment of eternal bondage? By that logic, Flavia once said to me in her mischievous way, he should have demonized all Romans and condemned them to eternal bondage on account of Pontius Pilate, I mean, he was the one who was responsible. As I studied the intelligent German in the plain suit on my right, the next question surged forward: how, as an intelligent German, does one manage to venerate a saint who, like no bishop before him, by justifying pogroms and hatred toward people of other faiths, ultimately may very well have provided the model for Hitler, Himmler, Kappler, and Co.? Or should one not construct such chains of associations from one mass of sin to the next, from Augustine to his disciple Luther to the Wannsee Conference to orders and the cruelty of following orders to conforming to the Jew-hatred inculcated in young men in black uniforms?

I tried with all my might to wipe the Nazi story from my mind, which always makes those of us who were born afterward run the risk of beating the little drum of trite accusations. Mind you, under other circumstances I seize every opportunity to address this question. Time and again I stand before my customers and say: You cannot understand Italy if you do not know about the wounds inflicted here in only twenty months between 1943 and 1945. One hundred sixty-five murders a day, not counting partisans, soldiers, and forced laborers killed. You cannot comprehend Rome if you do not feel the orders, the shots from our uniformed fathers, uncles, and grandfathers that remain lodged in the psyches, even of conciliatory Italians. That is why it always bristles, this history reflex, when German-speaking people—on the beach, at the cappuccino table, or posing for cameras—do not behave themselves, when they imperiously flaunt their blondness, become patronizing, or even when they cautiously and considerately address something uncomfortable or venture to criticize an evil that Italians themselves criticize, then it comes flying out, this reflex, sometimes silently, sometimes quietly, sometimes loudly: You and your Hitler! Shut up!

The two taunting syllables of this name cannot be erased from the memory of the peoples of the world. This curse is the price we have to pay for the hatred and obedience of our fathers and grandfathers, that has become clear to me in my twenty-seven years in Italy and twenty-four years with Flavia, a comparatively small price for so much hatred and obedience. It is precisely in Rome that this must not be forgotten, where one of those murderers, a smiling old man, is still running around in the spring of 2011, as I explain to my listeners when we're standing on the appropriate spot. The second-highest SS man in Rome, a torture specialist who was involved in the deportation of the Jews and later in the revenge killing of three hundred thirty-five Romans and then was able to hide in Argentina with the aid of the Vatican, he takes a walk with a police escort almost every day around the Villa Doria Pamphili, to the supermarket, to church, a retiree almost a hundred years old, under house arrest, and is applauded by the Italian fascists, who hail him on their Internet sites and almost succeeded in obtaining his services as a judge for the "Miss Destra" contest. The man himself is unimportant, I always point out, even though so much history is concentrated in his hands. You just ought to know that a few ghosts are still running around, very much alive, under this paradise-blue sky and that more people's minds than we may realize are still under occupation by uniformed ghosts.

For example, time and again I see Kappler's ghost haunting the city, not only in Via Tasso near the Lateran, where his SS tortured, right behind the Holy Stairs, within earshot of the Sancta Sanctorum chapel, not only in front of the synagogue, where he extorted and arrested, not only in Via Appia, where he murdered. The Italy connoisseur in SS uniform, he also haunts the area around the Colosseum, on the Celio, in front of the military hospital, whence, as a heavily guarded and gravely ill murderer sentenced to life in prison, under a clear night sky, he was supposedly lowered from the fourth floor by a German-Italian rock climbing team and spirited away to Germany in the terror year 1977. A classic Roman miracle that has remained unknown, the rappelling miracle of Monte Celio in the night before the Assumption of the Virgin Mary and the feast of Saint Alypius, who once upon a time brought stud-horses to Ravenna.

And no German pope, I tell the foreigners I guide, no Michael Schumacher, who won one world championship after another for Ferrari, no Goethe, the most successful tourist decoy of all time, is of any help. German-Italian understanding, as the politicians and diplomats tell us in honeyed voices, will always be difficult. Even our most agile soccer players, even if they have Turkish names and play for Italian clubs, are "panzers" in this country. Alaric and Adolf and Kappler and Kesselring—the destroyer of Florence and slaugh-terer of partisans—are not easily disposed of. Flavia pardons me for Alaric, at least, she knows her history. We Romans, she says, build this wonderful big wall, the Aurelian Wall, which everyone admires to this day, but we're too dumb to put soldiers on it when the Goths come and waltz right into the city—so ok, I give you a pass for Alaric. But Benito and Adolf, they're of a different caliber, they will cast their shadows for a long time to come.

We Germans like to tell ourselves, I sometimes say when I'm in a *ristorante* with a group (you can book me for that, too: background talks over spaghetti and osso buco), we Germans think we're doing something to improve relations with Italy just because we believe we're breathing the air of Caesar or Raphael and blithely put way too much parmesan on our noodles as we sit outside little trattorias. We think we're doing something for so-called understanding just because we

don't run around the black cobblestones in jackboots
and lockstep and are not as uniform as those big Asian
tour groups or the Rome-in-four-hours tourists that
they truck in from cruise ships at Civitavecchia and
because we politely say *buon giorno* and can pronounce
"espresso" more or less without an accent, better than
the Americans, anyway.

But we achieve no understanding, we understand
nothing at all if we do not understand the history, the
hot, volcanic pavement of history. Goethe thought one
needed to be up on three thousand years of it, I offer
two thousand, with a thousand gaps, of course. Our
ancestors were conquerors a little too often, and on top
of that we're atoning along with the Austrians, who
are also called *tedeschi*. The worst name they have for
us, *crucchi*, comes from starving Croatians in Austrian
uniforms crying for bread during the First World War.
All those things are charged to our account. Warriors,
plunderers, occupiers, and, as if that were not enough,
we're bad at concealing our tendency to assert our inner policeman in this country and—sometimes quietly,
sometimes more loudly—we demand rules. In traffic,
the traffic cop in us comes alive. On the train, taking out
the garbage, in the bank, at the post office, in government offices, we could instantly and with good reason
start in with the inspector or auditor. When there's tax
fraud, the finance cop wants to step in, in every new
case of corruption, the truth cop wants to go to work.
Mine gets worked up, too, time and again, my inner
guardian of order, so it's a good thing I have a wife
who can laugh about it. Even the German next to me on
the marble pew, I thought next, who seems to be resting and relaxing, as if he didn't have enough problems
already, has appointed himself policeman and judge
and wants to restore order and have the last word
on an Italian predecessor who protected criminals

and the persecuted alike and who excommunicated Communists en masse but not a single fascist—the last word: beatified.

We can do whatever we want, I often say, but to Italians and especially to Romans we are Germanic, and we've been the culprits ever since the Germanic tribes. We invaded Italy—more than once, in the guise of Goths, landsknechts, Nazis—and defiled Rome, no doubt about it. What the French, the Spanish, the Habsburgs, and countless incompetent popes have done to this country, often no less brutal, that doesn't count. The most useful enemy is, well, us, Ladies and Gentlemen, you, every one of you. Take the *Sacco di Roma*, 1527. The Catholic emperor, the Habsburg Spaniard Carl V, attacks the pope, who had provoked him, with fourteen thousand German, five thousand Spanish, and two thousand Italian landsknechts, who plunder Rome more thoroughly than it's ever been plundered before. Because most of the German landsknechts more or less sympathized with Luther, and because one of them carved the latter's initials on the Vatican, and although the Italians and gold-mad Spaniards rampaged no less savagely, and because the Swiss Guards—who at the time were still Protestant—protected the pope, in the end it is not the Catholics, not the Spanish, not the Catholic emperor, but the Germans, the Protestants, who are considered the worst barbarians. Eight years later, that same Carl, who almost went down in history as the murderer of a pope, is received in Rome by Paul III with full honors. That, well, that's politics, and politics means "forget." Only one thing is still certain: we Germans get the referee's hip-pocket penalty card, the "ass card," pardon the expression. We're just the culprits, plain and simple.

And we Italians, says Flavia, if we really want to include everyone, always feel we're victims; in every life situation, *siamo vittimisti*, says she. Even though our parents were fascist twice as long as yours were, even though ours killed half a million or a whole million people in Ethiopia, Libya, Greece, and the Balkans, not just as soldiers but in concentrations camps, too, with poison gas, mass shootings, and by deliberate starvation. There were so many victims of Mussolini's wars, at any rate, that seventy years on there is still no accurate count. Maybe it was zero point six million plus some, maybe one point one million, the number is not the main thing now. For me it's about the feeling of guilt: zero point zero. So many zeros, so much nothing, that they don't tell school children anything about it, older students only if they ask. No one talks about it, not even left and liberal journalists, no one. Our sins have never even been confessed, all the more reason that you guys will go on being used as culprits, because there's no doubt that your parents supplied the worst ones and also because it's so wonderfully convenient for us to be victims. Turning culprits, scoundrels, into innocent lambs, in this discipline our men are particularly hard to beat. Gold, silver, or bronze, every one of them sports some kind of medal on his chest. No one wants to be responsible, they all think they're innocent, and when things go wrong—and things usually do—you'll never hear mea culpa! When that happens, then the referee is to blame, or the judge, or the government. Or the Germanic peoples.

Sinner and scapegoat at the same time, you make the ideal combination, indispensable in a country where, she says derisively, people let themselves be ruled by a party of thieves, *Partito dei Ladri*, the PDL, hoodlums, robbers, liars, who are actually proud of being hoodlums, robbers, and liars. And before one of our thugs confesses to anything, he'll point a finger, shake his fist, shout curses at everyone else: the court system, the state, and, if that doesn't do it, at the Germanic tribes or the ruling German woman. Every ultrademocratic German, Flavia blasphemes, has to expect to get a Hitler mustache painted on his or her face, simply because this country cannot be reformed, cannot get the hang of running a functioning constitutional democracy and willingly lets itself be ruled and led around by the nose by a friend of the Mafia. And after he and his gang have run the country into the ground, once again nobody will be to blame, neither he nor his bought members of parliament and most assuredly not the people who elected him. Then the index finger will swing back to the north like a magnetic needle, you can bet your life on it.

We can try as hard as we want to become European brothers and sisters, I tell my good Germans, we can sing as many paeans as we like to the land of the most marvelous and diverse landscapes, with the best climate, the even better food, the finest fish restaurants, and the most beautiful women, we can praise the oleander from morning till midnight, the gorgeous décolletage, the sound constitution, the Mediterranean temperament, the fountains, the nice southern people, the capable president, the baristas' dances in front of their coffee machines, the figs, the wonderful piazzas, the September sun, the fashions. We can rave about the Italian morning light and the evening breeze and offer up all our favorite clichés in the finest gift wrap, we'll still be the Huns, the conquerors, admired but unloved, the panzers, for at least the next hundred years. And so, Ladies and Gentlemen, don't think you can refurbish relations between our countries by smiling back bravely at the waiters.

That's how my brain played these motifs for me like
an orchestra, melodies and variations on so-called love
for Italy in higher and lower registers, useful misunderstandings in fast and slow tempos, and sentimental
songs about red sunsets and dark, rainy, watercolor
skies, the eternal struggle between major and minor,
the earthly and the divine, facts and miracles. In Rome,
you're supposed to marvel at the miracles, and yet my
German mind, my Bremen mind, always wants to track
down as much truth as possible and preserve the dignity of the doubter. The city lives by its legends, and I
live by illuminating a few of them for my clientele. I
could not have allowed myself a nicer contradiction,
cannot imagine a better lot, and now, with three representatives of the miracle faction, three keepers of the
legends sitting almost beside me, apparently with nothing to do and making no move to leave, I did not want
to miss the opportunity to indulge in more questions
from the storehouse of miracles.

Calcata, this image, too, leaped into my mind and belongs in the record of the afternoon. What became of
the relic of Calcata, the foreskin of the boy Jesus? After
being venerated for centuries in the Sancta Sanctorum,
the private chapel of the popes at the top of the Holy
Steps, then getting lost during the *sacco di Roma*, then
being miraculously rediscovered, it was put on display
and worshipped in Calcata in Viterbo. How many pilgrims came to the cathedral in Calcata because of it
until, recently, it was secretly removed to a hiding place
in Rome or buried deep in the archives, as if to say that
today's faith is no longer sufficient for all miracles, as
though they wanted to hear and know nothing more
of the two-millennia-spanning adventure novel that
this body part could tell. Who was allowed to have the
say about such difficult things as circumcisions, Jewish
customs, to say yes or no to certain relics? Who makes

the decisions about such sacred body parts? Why are the severed heads of two warring apostles displayed in the Lateran, and why, in Santa Croce, are the finger of doubting Thomas and thorns from the crown of Him who was crucified on display but not the boy's equally real foreskin?

Silly questions, I knew, wrong, impermissible, improper questions. The art of doubting is not wanted, enlightenment not a goal under clear or rain-darkened skies of Rome, that is one lesson that all foreigners, especially the Germanic ones, would do well to learn when they're guests and then up and start meddling. Their place is to like the improbable and unbelievable, to be grateful and meekly draw from the fund that the capital of legends, fairy tales, and myths offers. The truth is not important, it is overrated. For that there is the *bocca della verità*, where tourists from all over the world stand in line and with their right hands or their left show that they are not liars and that there are no more liars in the world. The maw of truth, the maw of lies swallows everything, everything is swallowed and digested, horses included, whole horses, whole boatloads of horses. And again they stormed toward me, the stallions of the Bishop of Hippo, as though they too wanted to go to the great maw of truth. I tried to hold them back by the reins.

They galloped through the fields of my mind and, at the same time, because I willed it, down my Roman pathways, the ancient stallions or their progeny of who-knows-what horse generation since 418. I roamed the streets with my memory camera, panned across the enormous team of horses atop the Altar of the Fatherland towering high above the highest rooftops, to the quadriga at the Palace of Justice, to Garibaldi's gigantic steed and the wild one his wife Anita rides on the Janiculum, Saul's nag by Caravaggio, collected the horses adorned with water wings leaping from the rocks of the Trevi fountain, the sea horses and the Umberto stallion in the Villa Borghese, added Marcus Aurelius, valiant slayer of Germanic tribes, on his horse, and the Dioscuri, Castor and Pollux, the riding twins, the ur-gods of Rome, who have a temple in the Forum and sculptures on the Capitoline and on the Quirinal, the Monte Cavallo.

It all fit, I liked it, I was already starting to think of tours for horse lovers, for customers of means, ads in the equestrian press. A hole in the market: telling the story of the city through horses, from Castor and Pollux, the tutelary gods of riders, to the barracks where the oil dictator from Libya put his thoroughbreds through their paces—for the usual base reasons—then back for a show of the sacred stallions presented on the steps in front of Sant'Agostino. But whether you love horses or not, you have to admit that the worthy animals have had their day in the Eternal City. A dozen police horses don't count, the few remaining jades pull coaches with elderly foreigners and honeymooners through the hell-ish traffic, and at Carnival they trot out a few horses for show on the Piazza del Popolo for the sake of nostalgia. This is the epoch of dogs, rats, giant seagulls, and red palm beetles. Horses exist only out in the country or in ceiling paintings, plunging with the sun god's chariot.

If I were more courageous and better at educating the eye, I could point out the invisible horses behind every painting of Mary, in the background of history, bewilder audiences by asking whether there would be a cult of Mary, whether there would be all those images of the Mother of God, whether the Column of the Immaculate Conception on the Spanish Steps would even exist without the stallions and original sin.

Both are results of a council in 431, as one would have to explain to those curious about such details. Once the translators had turned the young Hebrew woman into a Greek virgin (in the Septuagint, I could say to the educated ones), after the famous Jerome, in translating the book of Luke from Greek into Latin (in the Vulgate), had taken Mary's gracefulness—Luke called her "graceful"—and appended "full of grace," *gratia plena*, to her name, the way was paved for her rise to virginal Mother of God, 431 years after the birth of her boy. Jesus could not be born of sinful flesh like everyone else, so he needed a virgin mother. "Birthgiver of God" was decided upon at the same council at which the concept of original sin and the banishment of Eros from the church were forced through. An interesting swap—a paradigm shift, academics would say—at a council that did not go off without sword, blackmail, and exclusion, Ephesus, in case you want to know more precisely, Ladies and Gentlemen. Miracles everywhere you look.

The fingers stirred, lay for a moment spread out on the black fabric on the thighs. The elderly gentleman got up very slowly, upper body bent forward. I saw him slightly stooped at first, then upright, strikingly erect, and after him his two escorts got up. He turned his head approximately in my direction, as though the horses or my heretical thoughts had provoked the movement, but he did not look far enough to the left to allow an exchange of glances. Although reason told me that he was not looking for me and that the change from a sitting to a standing posture could have nothing to do with me, I hoped for the first moment of a split second that he wanted to continue the conversation, which wasn't one yet, at the place to which I had transported us in my imagination, at a neutral location, on the steps in front of Sant'Agostino in the bracing early

March air, in the flattering afternoon sunlight, on that square jammed with cars, unencumbered by etiquette. And in the second split second I thought maybe, before making his way out the door, he wanted to end the unhoped-for encounter with a good, solid handshake to refute my archaeological speculations and interrupt the unbridled flights of my associations.

No one else got up, I didn't either, only the two escorts flanking him were standing. I watched him, sidelong as before, with the slow-motion gaze I'd become used to, not counting the seconds and tenths of a second, not aware of the minutes. The passage of time did not interest me, and I still could not have told you whether we had been sitting so close to each other for two minutes or twenty. In addition to the hands, I now studied the posture of the slim figure and dared not guess where his next steps might go. No minister in authoritative robe appeared to greet this visitor or bid him farewell, the psalm reader still had not finished or was reading his text for the third or fourth time, no one interrupted him, no one took over for him, the organ was silent, too, everything seemed slightly out of kilter or guided by deliberate irregularity.

Standing, viewed from the side, he didn't cut a bad figure, a better one, in any case, than did his immediate predecessor, who had only recently been resurrected in the form of a newly dedicated monument on the square in front of the railroad station, near the bus stops. A botched statue of a man soon to be beatified, vehemently criticized, even by the servile local press. A head that looks slow-witted, more like Mussolini's than that of the famous pope, rests on a cape resembling a bronze barrel, wide open at the front and of massive ugliness. What was probably meant to represent the protective, helping mantle of the church looked like a cold metallic cavity, and what was conceived as a person with papal authority was reminiscent of an exhibitionist drawing the attention of travelers and bus passengers to his wide-open cloak, to his empty inner life. Created by an artist close to the church, financed by a religious foundation, received as a gift by Rome's semi-fascist mayor, consecrated by a cardinal, the dilettantism of it made Romans grumble nonetheless, those loyal to the church and those critical of it. The monument stands as an example of the blasphemy of the superpious, of well-nigh heretical amorphousness, one big expression of angst, as I say on tours, a product of anemic opportunism, not Christian, artistic, or fascist, yet with a bit of each daubed on in uncommon ugliness.

He, however, was standing, erect and alive, without mantle, his head uncovered, in front of the marble pew. He did not have to pose for monuments, there was no fault to be found about him. The hands stirred, he moved the left one forward, curled it into a fist, relaxed it, the right hand repeated the discreet movements, then both reverted to the curved, inward-turned attitude of lurking inactivity and stubborn caution. Standing, he looked stronger, but, although he seemed closer, I felt the separation more than I had before, the ever-widening circles of distance that surrounded him, even without the armor of his vestments, and I thought: Somehow the good man has lost his way, gotten lost on his way to heaven and finds himself standing around perplexed in this Protestant church. But maybe that was not it at all and he was gathering his thoughts and looking outside his domain—almost recklessly, on enemy territory—for a little variety, recuperation, some breathing space.

Something in his sad look, perhaps also the air of anxiousness about him, reminded me, quite inappropriately,

of the great heretic on the other monument, Giordano
Bruno. I like to quote his statement about fear at
Campo de' Fiori when it's time for a five-minute talk
on the story of this monk who was burned alive, of his
denunciation and murder by the Inquisition: "Perhaps
you who pronounce my sentence are more afraid than
I who receive it." But my powers of observation, which
revolved around the standing pope, did not want to
go to Bruno. Everything about that rebellious monk is
known, and getting upset is gratuitous, you just need
to explain it to tourists briefly and be done with it. As
an encore, perhaps, in the sixth minute, touch on the
comedy that in 1929 the Curia wanted to see the monument to the most honorable of all heretics removed
with the help of Mussolini, whom they fawned over as
a "Man of Providence." When that didn't work, they
elevated Bruno's murderer-inquisitor Bellarmine, who
gagged Galileo as well, to sainthood and Doctor of the
Church—in the middle of the twentieth century. All
because of the proposition that the universe is infinite.
That's what I mean by comedy, Ladies and Gentlemen,
when angst and madness and truth, pretensions and re-
ality, emotions and facts, thought control and freedom
of thought yawn so gloriously far apart.

And the comedy doesn't end when you've discovered it
and ask what good the thousands of trials of so-called
heretics did, all the burnings, banishings, excommuni-
cations, all the wars of religion and brilliant intrigues.
Fear of the world, of the present, of intelligence, of
being contradicted, of thinking, still has not been
eliminated. Even if disobedient monks are no longer
burned, think of all the carefully chosen Latin words
that have been marshalled to brand freedom of con-
science, freedom of opinion, and democracy the work
of the devil, how they've twisted and turned to retract
some of it halfway decades later. All in vain. Fear of

the world, of the warmth and diversity of intelligence has grown steadily. Even the invention of infallibility and the claim to being right all the time, the certainty of possessing the only key to salvation and for opening heaven's door, have become more like a trap and have not made a bad world better.

I thought my archaeologist's eye could detect traces of such anxiety in the grieving hands, too, in the sad look, a sort of fear of fear. Something had happened, some rift in an overburdened soul. He too, this powerful man, together with his powerful institution, felt he was a victim—you could read about it—a victim of the media, of egalitarianism, of misunderstandings, of the general relativism, oddly, however, never of the ruling relativizer of law and order and morals, the self-appointed liberator from sin and punishment. This good man, I mused, might much prefer to have been pope in a time, such as a hundred and eighty years ago, when one could still raise to the dignity of sainthood a monk who, upon spying roasted larks on the plate of an epicure of a Friday, recalled the birds to life so that they could fly out the window, fledged and happy, thereby preventing a violation of the Friday ban on meat. Or when Pius IX could take the time to dilate for pages upon whether male embryos have a soul on the fortieth day after conception whereas female embryos get one only on the eightieth.

Something toppled. From the rightmost corner of my eye I saw something fall and thought, before I had switched back to full awareness, of a falling monument, Bruno's monument at Campo de' Fiori or that of John Paul at the railway station, a bronze figure tilting forward, a monk or a pope, I was seized with the fear that massive statues were falling in slow motion, as though there had been an earthquake in the area. For a moment

I had not paid attention, lost myself in images and dizzily whirling contradictions, failed to keep my eye on the hands. I didn't see the movement plainly, but I felt it, I sensed in a flash of panic that someone was falling, from weakness, fainting, falling forward, just as I had fainted and fallen forward onto the sidewalk on Via Salaria years ago at the entrance to a shoe store before losing consciousness for a few seconds.

So at first I saw only myself fall in a delayed reliving of that moment, now accelerated by fearfulness: a slight dizziness, a panicky dizziness, your legs give out, your arms reach out as you fall, vainly clutching for support, no tree, no column to grab, not even a lamppost. First the dizziness, irresistible dizziness, you try to cushion the fall, not let head and body strike the ground, the uncontrollable fainting, finally the solid asphalt of Via Salaria or, in this case, ecclesiastical marble.

But it was not I who was falling to the ground, it was the famous elderly gentleman, who had been standing a few meters to my right, who had dropped, not in a dizzy fainting spell like mine, but face forward onto the floor in the center aisle, and though his limbs were spread evenly, lay there as though he'd had an accident, the way no healthy grown man should be lying. I was alarmed, no, really concerned that something might have happened to him, heart, circulation, convulsions. I was sorry, it hurt me to see the old man in such weakness. My imagination immediately readied the bier, the coffin, the solemn, pompous farewell. I got up. For the first time in these two minutes or twenty I was standing, I wanted to go over and offer to help in some way, but the two escorts knelt beside him and seemed competent enough. There was no defense against the force of the thought: if he dies now, if the pope dies in a Protestant church, the absurdity of it would be almost unbearable for Catholics, too much for anyone, a humiliation, a gigantic embarrassment.

I didn't want that, I didn't want to be witness to such a sensation, yet I was already a witness, heard sirens, the sirens of ambulances, ever louder, ever closer, just as years ago I had been relieved to hear them when my eyes reopened and my head was being supported, surrounded by sympathetic passersby on Via Salaria, as an ambulance plowed through the evening traffic to scoop me up from the sidewalk and assure curious onlookers that everything was all right and help was at hand. Still, I did not want to witness a scene like that, the head of a church, prostrated by infirmity, lying at my feet, and I thought: How fortunate that no cameras are flashing and that everyone is being disciplined and remaining in their places.

The hands that I had practiced watching for so long stirred to life, flexed, and spread. The elderly gentleman pushed himself up, bent his arms, his legs, the escorts helped him regain his balance. I finally realized that he, quite unlike me in my fainting spell, had dropped to the ground intentionally, lain down on the marble floor and perhaps had touched or kissed it in veneration. Like his famous predecessor, who, when he was in a foreign country, as soon as he got off the plane, used to kiss the ground or the concrete apron of an airport, he had thrown himself to the floor of this church as though he had just landed. Only now, for the first time, as he was getting up with assistance on two sides, did I see where his head had been: close to the engraved, blackened capital letters on a light stone slab. I took two short steps to the right, and in the inscription thought I could make out the letters L and U and T side by side in a row.

No, I cannot swear he kissed them, the letters of the
name of the Reformer, I cannot swear that he deliber-
ately kissed them or only brushed them or did not touch
them at all, I am not a reliable witness to the possible
historic moment of a reverent movement of the lips.
What I saw clearly was only his body, his face toward
the ground in a sort of prostrate bow to these letters,
this name. And I did not know immediately what to
make of it, because first my fears had to be allayed.
The sirens of the ambulances were no longer audible,
the fear dissipated that a visit to the emergency room
might turn into a nightmare for the elderly gentleman
like the one I had experienced. All the intervention of
paramedics and emergency-room personnel that my
overly hasty brain had anticipated melted away. In my
initial fright I had completely forgotten that this patient,
as the most privileged of the privileged, would have
been treated quite differently than I had been in the
stifling, bacteria-laden ward, crammed with the injured,
the moaning, the bleeding, the dying, with new arrivals,
the forgotten or seemingly forgotten, with the shouting, agitated families of the sick, with emergency-room
patients pleading incessantly for medical attention in
the Umberto hospital.

He was spared a trip like that, which in the end
bestowed upon me or cursed me with premature retirement (but that is another matter, a private one),
and that was such a relief that at first what had just
happened—or might have happened while my imagination was playing the short film about the dizzy spell
to its embarrassing conclusion—did not register. In the
split-second tempo of my thoughts it seemed a very
long time before I realized that this infallible man had
bowed before Luther. Before Luther! That was going
too far for my taste. Luther was no saint, moreover, he
was an Augustinian with heavy original-sin baggage.

But I was not there as an arbiter of good taste or as a representative of the Council but as an accidental observer and a self-appointed critic of papal hands. Before anything else I had to comprehend and sustain the strange act of submission that I had just seen.

He was standing again, smoothed his suit, adjusted the stiff, white collar, his companions tugged here and there. He seemed composed, what little movement there was in his features might have presaged a smile. As absurd as it was, I had to think of Bernini's elephant: "It takes a strong mind to sustain solid wisdom." A pope bows, throws himself to the ground before Luther. Strong minds should be able to sustain such a sight. Why should a miracle like this not happen in a city in which the laws of probability count for little, epiphanies and visions are built into the foundations, and genuflections carry more weight than the norms of reason and capricious common sense? Even the lord of Roman fairy tales, myths, legends, and visions himself could for once become an active participant in a miracle or illumination.

It was with self-soothing formulas like these that I watched Rome's most stared-at man, now stared at by me, too, as he strode purposefully to the pulpit, as though he finally wanted to say something, clarify something, and as though he had no time to waste. I hoped for a concluding word on galloping studhorses or about the unfathomable malice of nihilism or an explanation for the unprecedented gesture, the prostration performed with such matter-of-course calm before the name beginning with L. What I had seen, however, was about to be surpassed by what I heard.

He ascended the narrow steps to the pulpit with the eagle lectern, withdrew neither a breviary nor notes from his jacket, rested both arms, both hands, on the parapet. The left hand, the right hand, both were back in service. He drew a breath and, with no other introduction, let these words resound throughout the great space: "A mighty fortress is our God," each syllable spoken forcefully, not sung. A dramatic pause lent emphasis to the statement. I thought he was referring to the psalm that had been read, in which firmness, fortresses, and castles were mentioned, that he intended to give it his own interpretation and launch into a sermon, but he continued: "a trusty shield and weapon." Pause. "He helps us free from every need." Pause. "That hath us now overtaken." He recited the entire hymn, word for word, with a short pause after each line to emphasize the text.

My first reaction: This is truly a Roman miracle! You must tell Flavia! And the second: You underestimated him, he is definitely shrewder than you, in these two or twenty minutes he has done more reflecting than you were able to see. While you were probing thoughts that he was not thinking behind that forehead, speculating about the slaps not given and unwhispered declarations of love, while you were ascribing inexperience to those hands, maybe he had summoned all his rationality or faith and decided that everything would be simpler if he himself became a Lutheran. An ingenious solution, to step out of the centuries-old role and with one bold stroke to shake off many or most of the problems that he and his apparatus have to grapple with, which daily become more complicated and can be overcome neither with the traditional method of beatification nor that of condemnation, neither with the need to be right all the time nor with rituals made for TV. And yet, with Luther, to remain true to his cherished original sin. A genius! I thought, not knowing whether genius is allowed in theology. The church has always been capable of change, as the saying goes, otherwise it could not have survived for two thousand years, and, one might add, if an entire church, with the aid of eighty studhorses, can be bent one hundred eighty degrees, to the perversion of original sin, then maybe it can negotiate lesser curves without horses or comparable gifts.

With his voice, the words of the hymn acquired the gentle, sustained force of a confession of faith, precisely because the man who spoke them had stayed quiet the whole time and politely held back. Pay close attention, I told myself after the second stanza, listen to each syllable, every accentuation. Whether you want to or not, you will be needed as a witness to this event on the Shrove Sunday before Rose Monday and Ash Wednesday. If anyone should dispute that the elderly gentleman in the black suit really recited the Lutheran hymn fervently, this text with all its verses, in a trained voice, into precisely adjusted microphones, loudly and with the light of certainty, with the same intonation he uses for his Easter and Christmas messages on St. Peter's Square, you will have to bear witness to it, whether you want to or not.

Only now do I regret that no cameras were present, but it never occurred to me to turn on my cell phone and set it to record mode to capture a shaky video clip and at least the original soundtrack of the fourth verse. Perhaps it was reluctance to spoil this astonishing, solemn moment with graphic exploitation, a moment in which Luther's words were heard from the mouth of a pope as though a profession of faith. When he had spoken the fourth stanza, from "The Word," pause, "they shall," pause, "let remain" to "The Kingdom our remaineth," and sealed it with a discreet smile of relief, he descended the steps with measured tread, evidently expecting neither applause nor whistles, strode to the exit with his escorts, waved neither his left hand nor the right, and disappeared from my sight.

I dashed out after him into the early March air, almost alarmed by what I had seen and heard, alarmed in a way that I could not explain to myself, and saw a limousine with a flashing blue light at the end of Via Sicilia turn into Via Veneto, toward the wall, toward Byron, the shortest route to the Vatican. As I was phoning Flavia, who had just boarded the Eurostar in Milan, the woman with the little amore dog crossed the street and opened the door of a house. Flavia did not laugh at me, she believed me, and that was reassuring. I was eager to tell her everything, but I had to force myself to be patient a few more hours. Now, for the first time, I looked at my watch. The encounter with the high visitor could not have lasted more than five to eight minutes.

I continued my stroll, and the less I tried to make sense of what I had just seen, the more my alarm subsided, and, as I floated up the broad, flat steps of the Capitoline Hill, just for the fun of it, I found it again, the beauty, the rhythms of the city. I felt how easily the different tempos of looking, breathing, walking, and thinking fit together. I didn't look for them, these beats, they whirred from every side, they vibrated under every stone, and once again I knew that you can go forward and backward at the same time, simultaneously look at something and look away, think and repress, upload and download, descend as you ascend and ascend as you descend, and breathe in the beauty, inhale it deeply. Then, in Santa Croce, as though nothing at all had happened, I showed the people from Heilbronn the finger of doubting Thomas and told his story with well-routined humor.

That same evening, March 6, 2011, though she was exhausted from the trip and the conference, Flavia listened to me with growing interest. She encouraged me to write down the unbelievable encounter, down to its deepest layers, including the entire procession of my thoughts. Write down, she said, as objectively and accurately as you can, what your ears heard and your eyes saw. That same night I began setting down the first pages of my draft. The news reported that the oil dictator was moving against peaceful demonstrators with tanks and antiaircraft rockets. About the most important event in Rome, not a word.

On Friday, February 8, 2013, the present, final version of this book was sent from Rome by e-mail to the publisher in Berlin at 4:59 p.m. February 10 was Shrove Sunday. On the following day, Monday, February 11 at 11:46 a.m. the news came that the pope would resign his office on February 28, 2013.　　　　　F. C. D.

© juergen-bauer.com

## *About the Author*

Friedrich Christian Delius was born in Rome in 1943 and grew up in Central Germany. He did his doctoral thesis in German studies in 1970 and subsequently worked as book editor. Today he divides his time between the Italian capital and Berlin. Some of his best-known works are *Ribbeck's Pears* (1991), *The Sunday I Became World Champion* (1994), *The Walk from Rostock to Syracuse* (1995), and *My Year as a Murderer* (2004). *Portrait of the Mother as a Young Woman* (2006) was translated into English by Jamie Bulloch for Peirene Press in 2010. Delius has won numerous awards, including the German Critics' Prize, the Joseph Breitbach Prize, and the highly prestigious Georg Büchner Prize.                www.fcdelius.de

## *About the Translator*

Bob Cantrick grew up in the United States and attended the University of Rochester and the Johannes Gutenberg University in Mainz, earning a BA degree in German. He did graduate work at the universities of Cologne and Bonn on a fellowship then continued studies in Germanic languages and literature at Indiana University (Bloomington) on a teaching assistantship. Among many other things, he has worked as a freelance translator, in-house translator and editor, and legal secretary-translator. Since 2015 he has concentrated on literary translation.

In 2016 he was one of the winners of the New Books in German Translation Competition. In 2017 he won second prize in the John Dryden Translation competition. In 2018 he was one of the featured translators at the *Festival Neue Literatur* in New York City.

He is retired and lives in Toronto.